KT-157-897

‖‖‖ ‖‖‖ ‖ ‖‖‖‖‖‖ ‖‖‖ ‖‖‖‖‖‖ ‖‖‖ ‖‖‖‖ ‖‖ ‖‖‖

ACTION AT ARCANUM

At their Bar-V C ranch in Arizona, Vance Callister and his wife Anne are found dead. The evidence indicates a murder-suicide and there is excited speculation in Arcanum City. The problem is: Who died first? If it was Vance, his daughter is disinherited; if Anne died first, her brother and sister lose.

Gregory Quist, the famous detective, investigates, to the accompaniment of more shootings and mysterious goings-on, and at last brings the case to its complicated and bloody conclusion.

(Allan) William Colt MacDonald was born in Detroit, Michigan in 1891. His formal education concluded after his first three months of high school when he went to work as a lathe operator for Dodge Brothers' Motor Company. His first commercial writing consisted of advertising copy and articles for trade publications. While working in the advertising industry, MacDonald began contributing stories of varying lengths to pulp magazines and his first novel, a Western story, was published by Clayton House in *Ace-high Magazine* in 1925. MacDonald later commented that when this first novel appeared in book form as *Restless Guns* in 1929, 'I quit my job cold.' From the time of that decision on, MacDonald's career became a long string of successes in pulp magazines, hardcover books, films, and eventually original and reprint paperback editions. The Three Mesquiteers, MacDonald's most famous characters, were introduced in 1933 in *Law of the Forty-fives.* His other most famous character creation was Gregory Quist, a railroad detective. Some of MacDonald's finest work occurs outside his series, especially the well researched *Stir Up The Dust* which was published first in a British edition in 1950 and *The Mad Marshal* in 1958. MacDonald's only son, Wallace, recalled how much fun his father had writing Western fiction. It is an apt observation since countless readers have enjoyed his stories now for nearly three quarters of a century.

C0038 05983

ACTION AT ARCANUM

William Colt MacDonald

GUNSMOKE

First published in the UK by Hodder and Stoughton

This hardback edition 2007
by BBC Audiobooks Ltd
by arrangement with
Golden West Literary Agency

Copyright © 1958 by Allan William Colt MacDonald.
Copyright © 1961 by Allan William Colt MacDonald in
the British Commonwealth.
Copyright © renewed 1986 by Wallace MacDonald.
All rights reserved.

ISBN 978 1 405 68175 9

British Library Cataloguing in Publication Data available.

GLASGOW CITY LIBRARIES	
C003805983	
HJ	09/11/2007
FMAC	£9.95
	R

Printed and bound in Great Britain by
Antony Rowe Ltd., Chippenham, Wiltshire

IT IS possibly very true that an overindulgence in alcohol can be responsible for an extreme mental depression and jittery nerves. Particularly on the morning following such intemperance. It is a fact that the greater part of pledge cards are signed "the morning after." Not that Stovepipe Hudson had any intention of signing the pledge; the thought hadn't even occurred to him, even though he sensed something was bothering him, and he didn't like it. Not any of it. Maybe he was just halfway between a drunk and a hangover, at that point where a man's mind churns up unexplainable thoughts, where he thinks clearly, after a fashion, before descending to the maudlin point. No, there was no question of signing the pledge; again, morning was still many hours off. So it couldn't have been a hangover depression that bothered Stovepipe.

But worried he was, and jumpy; the least sound along the shadowed trail set his heart to beating faster. It was a sort of spooky night anyway, he considered, the kind that naturally made a man nervous. But there wasn't a thing he could put his finger on to explain his feelings. This was queer country anyway, he told himself, and he should never have left Texas in the first place. And all that talk tonight, back in the Gold Dollar Saloon, with the boys telling the old tales about the Arcanum country, and one of them even stating there were ghosts in the mountains. And these wheels squeaking behind, just set his teeth on edge.

The sense of despondency settled deeper, while he slumped on the seat of the buckboard, a rawboned individual with a long red nose, wide straggling mustaches and a battered slouch hat pulled low on his balding head. His skinny legs were encased in faded denims and his coat collar was turned up at the back of his neck. The reins were gathered loosely in one gnarled fist and the horses did little more than maintain progress, the wheels of the wagon scarcely stirring the dust of the trail that ran to the Box-VC Ranch.

Overhead, a gibbous moon moved sluggishly through broken cloud shapes. Shadows passed almost imperceptibly across jagged upthrusting rocks on either side of the trail. All about was a nearly flat vista of sand and sage and mesquite, with here and there a paloverde lifting above the lower plant growths. An ancient cottonwood just beyond an outcropping of black-spired rock rustled eerie leaves in the chill night breeze pushing steadily down from the serrated peaks of the Arcanum Mountains towering black, brooding, ominously silent, almost—it seemed—over Stovepipe Hudson's head, despite the fact they rose at least twenty miles distant.

Stovepipe lifted his head and eyed warily the silhouetted dark jagged peaks. To his hazy mind the mountains appeared to be closing in on him. A shudder coursed his spine. . . . "I know damn' well something bad's going to happen. Maybe it's already happened. It's like I got one of these here forebodin's of evil, or a premynition of death, or something. There's something up. I can feel it in the air—"

An owl sounded abruptly from a patch of mesquite, and Stovepipe jumped as though a gun had been fired in his ear. Chill shivers raised goose-flesh on the back of his neck before he realized it was only an owl that had startled him. He cursed in a trembling voice and irritably slapped the reins across the horses' backs.

"For gaw'sakes, pick up them hoofs, you spavined, gall-sored, broke-down, sons of no-good crowbaits!"

The horses quickened to a trot that lasted but a few minutes,

6

then again, unnoticed by Stovepipe, settled back to a walk, "Reckon where I made my mistake," he grumbled, "was not stayin' in town and getting drunk with the rest of the outfit. This quittin' halfway when a man ain't neither sober, nor yet wall-eyed tanked, just ain't no good. It's jus' the same as feedin' a man his sow-bosom and beans, and then tellin' him there ain't no apple pie—"

He interrupted his soliloquy to jerk his head around. For a minute there, he thought he'd heard the drumming of hoofs across the earth. Nope, must have been mistaken. Couldn't hear it now. If it was a rider, what was he doin' way off there? Any rider comin' this way would have sense enough to follow the trail.

And then, a second thought: "Though Gawd knows anything could happen the way I feel tonight. There was that talk of ghosts. Wonder if a man could hear a ghost's hawss." Stovepipe forced a nervous laugh. "There ain't no such things as ghosts, of course. Any sensible man knows that much. It's all fool talk to scare folks. Yep, I should have stayed in town and got me a real head-buster. Only for Vance actin' the way he did this mawnin' . . ."

Stovepipe got another thought. "Could be that's why I'm feel-ing lower'n a rattler's belly. Vance sure dressed me down. No sense of him getting so mad, nuther. Seven years now I cooked for his outfit and he never before handed me no such bawlin'-out. And for why? 'Cause I run short of Red Dawg. I could have told him his missus borried so much flour from me for her cakes and cookies, that I was bound to run short. She must have spoiled a heap of bakin'. Not that I'm a one to tell on a lady for her shortcomin's. And she never struck me neither, like some-body who could cook. And if the truth was knowed, maybe that's what caused his indigestion."

Shaking his head dolefully, Stovepipe spat out his cud of to-

7

bacco, fumbled in one pocket and produced a partially bitten plug. In the half light of the moon, he eyed the plug from all sides and bit off a fresh chunk. Again he urged the horses to a faster gait, but that didn't last long. He continued aggrievedly, "And just 'cause I want to accompany the boys to town for a little pay-day spree, he hits the ceiling. And I had a good excuse. I'd run short of flour. And then I'm ten kinds of a poor apology for a cook. Can't even keep supplies on hand. Now I asks you—" appealing to the range at large—"is that any reason for Vance gettin' so mad? Somebody has to stay in the bunkhouse, he says, to take care of things. What things? Ain't nobody goin' to steal the place. And should he want a snack, his missus, even if'n she can't bake, should know how to make coffee an'—By Gawd! There wa'n't no reason for him gettin' so mad at me. Better if he bawled out whoever was responsible for keepin' them hind wheels greased. All quiet for a spell, then sudden they screeches out like a wailin' banshee, scarin' a man nigh to death—" He paused suddenly, listening, sat straighter on the seat. "Damn' if that didn't sound like a shot!"

He strained his ears. Nothing to be heard except the rustling of leaves and the continual off-and-on squeaking of the rear wheels.

"Reckon I was mistook. Mebbe a rock busted loose in the mountains." He shook his head, mind still hazy from the drink he'd taken. "I sure am spooked. Nervy as an old maid in a parlor house. Got to get holt on myself, 'fore I go snappy like Vance. He's jest been testier'n a bobcat ever since he got tangled with them women. A man his age—his age—" The cook yawned, blinked drowsily. His words came slower, as his head dropped to his chest. There came a long drawn, raucous snore, so loud it jerked him awake. His heart beat madly.

"Was that a shot?" he gasped. He listened. Maybe he'd just dreamed he heard a shot. Or maybe them wheels squeaked extra loud. "Hell," he mumbled uneasily, "maybe it's just my 'magination. Who'd be shootin' over that direction. All the hands is still in town. Wouldn't be no call for Vance to be shootin' this time of night. Like's not he's in bed, anyway. 'Course, could be somebody from another outfit tooken too much liquor, fell asleep and his hawss strayed over this way. Then when he woke up he took a shot at the moon for good luck. Cripes! I'm just worryin' over nothin'. I'd just better get home soon's possible, give Vance this letter and hit the hay."

He straightened on the seat, slapped the reins smartly. The squeaking wheels sounded louder as he urged the horses to greater efforts.

The horses threw themselves into the traces, plunging ahead on the moon-shadowed road. When after a few minutes they again showed signs of decreasing pace, the cook reached for his whip and plied it vigorously. Hoofs thudded, harness jangled. Dust billowed up at the rear of the buckboard. Wheels jarred brutally on rocks imbedded in the roadway. Had there been any gunshots or hoofbeats now, the noise made by wagon and team would have drowned them out.

By this time the alcoholic haze that had clouded Stovepipe's mind began to clear, and though it wasn't now more than two miles to the ranch, an ever-increasing presentiment of something sinister permeating the night compelled him to arrive with no further loss of time.

The thought occurred: Perhaps something had gone wrong at the house. But what? What could go wrong? There was nobody but Vance and his missus there, and the boss had always had a rep for being able to take care of himself. But perhaps he really had heard shots. Stovepipe frowned. Hell, he couldn't be certain. Sort of groggy like he was—and anyway they seemed kind of far off.

A quarter mile farther on he skidded the wagon around the

9

last curve in the trail without decreasing speed. Now it was all straight going between long lines of cottonwoods that flanked the road on either side. The horses plunged on with no let-up. Stovepipe didn't slacken pace until the wide gateway, situated in a far stretching fence composed of pitahaya cactus, hove into view. The gate stood open, but that didn't mean anything. It was swung wide most of the time. Beyond lay the ranch yard and the various buildings. The steady clanking of the windmill sounded peaceful enough.

Stovepipe pulled the horses to a walk and drew a long breath. "Reckon I'm just a pinheaded ol' fool," he breathed his relief. "Too much imagination mixed with too much whisky—or maybe I didn't have enough liquor." His gaze took in the buildings, all dark at present, except the ranch house, a large one-storied building constructed of rock and adobe. Here, light shone from the windows, front and side, of the big main room.

"Looks like Vance is still up. Hope he's better-natured than he was this mornin'. Only I got this letter to deliver, I'd just ease myself into the bunkhouse and not approach him until the time looked right. But what's got to be has got to be."

He reined the team down past the house, glancing toward the lighted windows as he drove by, but couldn't see anyone. Just beyond the bunkhouse he brought the buckboard to a halt near one of the corrals, where a few saddlers stirred restlessly beneath the pallid light of the half-clouded moon. He stepped down from the wagon seat and somewhat reluctantly started to negotiate the forty-odd intervening yards to the back door of the ranch house.

His pace slowed as he neared the rear door. Again that feeling that all was not right overtook him. It was just too quiet hereabouts. By this time he should have caught some sound from the house—a voice, the scraping of a chair—something. "Quiet as a graveyard," Stovepipe muttered, and again that cold shiver ran down his spine. That simile was a bad choice. Stovepipe

10

didn't like to think of graveyards. Warily, he eyed the back of the house. It was all dark here. The back door was closed.

The cook approached and knocked timidly. There was no response. He knocked a second time. Louder. The sound echoed through the house, but there came no welcoming call to enter. Stovepipe's heart started to pound. "Hope—hope they ain't both gone to bed," he mumbled, and his voice wasn't quite steady. "Vance might be right riled was I to wake him up."

A third knock brought no reply.

Stovepipe stood frowning in the shadow of the house, pondering the matter. Could be, he'd been right. Maybe something had gone wrong. The back door stood closed. He tried the knob. The door was unlocked. It swung back easily under his hand.

The cook hesitated, peering down the long dark hall that ran the length of the house. Light shone through the nearly closed door leading into the main room, just a slim sliver of light.

Stovepipe raised his voice, "Hey, Vance—Mister Callister! I'm back. I—I got a letter for you."

His tones sounded unusually loud in the deathlike quiet of the house. There was no answer. Stovepipe swallowed hard. With an effort he raised his voice: "Anybody home in there?"

After a minute he quavered half aloud, "Reckon they must both have gone to town. I guess I'll just slip in and leave this letter on the table."

Stovepipe made no move to enter farther however. For no reason he could conceive, he felt shaky. Blood pounded in his ears. His knees felt weak. Cold tremors ran down his spine.

"I'm actin' like an old fool," he told himself. "There ain't nothin' to be scairt of. All's I got to do is go on straight along this hall, go in that front room, leave the letter and then head for the hay. Damn you, Stovepipe, shake those hoofs."

A certain aversion dogged his steps as he advanced into the hall, softly closing the door behind him. To his right was an

11

open door leading into the kitchen. All dark there, though a faint light entering from a window picked out a highlight on the kitchen stove. He continued on, walking on tiptoes though he didn't realize it.

At the entrance to the main room, he paused just opposite the sliver of light emerging past the nearly closed door.

"You in there, Vance?" he quavered.

By this time he didn't expect a reply. Cautiously he pushed open the door and peered within. At first nothing appeared unusual. A shaded oil lamp burned on the big oaken table. The chairs were large and comfortable and empty. Navajo rugs were placed about the floor.

"Yep, must have gone to town, I reckon," the cook mused. He began to breathe easier, pushed the door wider and stepped into the room. He was nearly to the table in the center of the floor, when his breath caught and he halted abruptly.

A gasp left his parted lips. He took one involuntary step back, then forced himself to round the corner of the table. A sudden trembling shook his rawboned frame, and he gazed as though hypnotized at the two silent figures sprawled on the floor.

"Good Gawd a'mighty!" Stovepipe exclaimed.

Vance Callister, a big man with graying hair, lay on his side, one knee drawn up, head resting on an outflung arm. Blood formed a coagulating pool beneath his body.

Only a few feet from the dead man lay the body of a woman on her face, one outstretched hand clutching a Colt six-shooter. There was a dark stain on her shirtwaist, her skirts were rumpled. Her ash-blond hair was tumbled about her head and shoulders.

Stovepipe Hudson realized suddenly that queer noises were issuing from his throat. One hand jerked to his mouth as though to stifle them. "By Gawd, I had the right hunch. There was somethin' wrong," he gasped, horror widening his eyes.

12

Trembling, he advanced closer, stooped and cautiously touched the bodies, one after the other. They didn't feel cold—not yet—but there was no doubt about it. Both man and woman were dead.

"Killed him and then shot herself," Stovepipe whispered. "Great Gawd in the mountains . . ."

His gaze had gone to Vance Callister's holster. It was empty.

The cook was already backing away before he realized it, moving faster with each retreating step. He bumped into the edge of the open door and something like a groan of terror broke from his lips. For just an instant he hesitated in the hall, and in that moment he thought he heard a slight noise.

That was enough to set him off. He wheeled and plunged blindly along the hall to the rear of the house and burst through the back door into the open. A loud yell for "Help!" burst from his lips before he realized there was no one else at the ranch.

Teeth chattering, he forced himself to enter the bunkhouse, get a saddle, then catch up a horse from the corral. The cinch was pulled tight with shaking hands. Then Stovepipe climbed up and headed the pony for town, beating the animal over the head in his frantic haste to get there and break the tragic news, mumbling over and over to himself, "I knowed there was somethin' wrong. I just knowed it."

II

GREGORY QUIST, Special Investigator for the Texas Northern & Arizona Southern Railroad, sat at his desk in his living quarters-office room on the second floor of El Paso's Pierson Hotel. The desk stood near open windows through which flowed early spring breezes, and warm sunshine. The remainder of the room was pleasantly furnished with a couple of straight-backed chairs

13

and one with arms. The bed was at the far side of the room. There was a dresser, commode and small mirror. A carpet covered the floor.

Quist's coat and a six-shooter in an underarm holster hung on the foot of the bed. There were three empty beer bottles in a wastepaper basket, two full ones stood on Quist's desk and from time to time he took sips from a third. Again he picked up the letter he'd been reading, frowning slightly over its contents.

Quist was a broad-shouldered individual in vest and corduroy trousers, flannel shirt, open at the throat. A shock of tumbled tawny hair covered his head. In a day and country in which most men wore beards or at least wide mustaches, Quist was clean-shaven, with a wide, thin-lipped mouth and features on the bony side. His amber-colored eyes—or were they topaz?—had a direct way of looking at a man. He held the reputation of being hard, ruthless, though even his worst enemies—and he'd made a lot of them in his time—never termed him anything but just.

For the second time he put down the letter he'd been reading, and gazed, meditatively, through one open window, across the rooftops of El Paso, where Franklin Mountain raised its peak against the cobalt sky. On the street below the hotel the jangling of a mule-drawn street car broke into Quist's thoughts, and he brought his attention back to the desk.

"Some people do get the damnedest ideas," he said aloud, the low resonant tones welling deeply from his chest. He laughed shortly. "Just because I've had a bit of luck on a few jobs this—what's his name, Bancroft?—must figure there's no limit to my capabilities. Jeepers! What he needs is a doctor, not a railroad dick. Or, maybe, two doctors, so they can draw out the argument, and thus increase fees. I doubt any railroad operative is going to be able to help him. Leastwise, not me. Well, he's entitled to a reply, I suppose, stating my regrets I can't handle his problem due to being under contract to the T.N. & A.S., and so

14

on and so on. . . ." He broke off, frowning, to reach for paper and pen. "I must say the fellow's well informed on the past jobs I've settled."

Momentarily, Quist's frown deepened, then he sighed and began writing. A few minutes later he placed his written refusal in an envelope and sealed it.

Steps sounded in the hall outside his door. A knock resounded against the wooden panel. Quist called, "Come on."

The door opened, closed again. Quist swung around in his desk chair to see a thin gray-haired man in rather rumpled town clothing standing there. The man had tired eyes behind rimless spectacles; he looked rather harassed.

"Thought I'd find you here," the man nodded shortly, "drinking beer as usual."

"As usual, Jay," Quist admitted cheerfully. "Spring weather calls for good beer, and the day is right warmish. I strolled over to your office, looking for you, an hour back. This heat makes the juices run—"

"I was called out for a time—"

"Will you join me in a bottle? You've been walking, too—"

Jay Fletcher made a grimace of revulsion. "You know I can't drink that slop, Greg. And you don't even ice it—"

"You're maligning the sacred name of beer, Jay. Slop your grandmother! And no sensible man wants ice-cold beer. Let me send down for some whisky—"

"Too early in the day for my drinking habits." Fletcher drew up a chair near the desk. "Look here, Greg, something important has come up and I think you can handle it. Things have been pretty quiet for you, lately, for which the company is grateful of course—"

"No flattery, please," Quist said dryly. "I can tell by your manner you're going to hand me a tough nut to crack."

Fletcher frowned impatiently. "I doubt it will be as tough as

15

that, Greg. I really don't think it should take long for a smart man—and a smart man is indicated in this matter that involves the welfare of the company—"

"Don't tell me," Quist jeered, "that anything threatens the well-being of our precious railroad. Are dividends threatened? Have some bad boys broken into a freight car and you want me to spank 'em? Or was some big stockholder deservedly murdered and you want me to run down his killer—"

"Damn it, Greg—" Fletcher scowled—"you're too blasted cynical. You always have been—"

"How could a man be anything but cynical on my job? Year after year I see the company making larger and larger profits. Your directors bleat of service to the public, but deep down you realize they don't give a damn about the public unless they make money for the stockholders. They never give a thought to the little men who work their hearts out, or to the people who are sometimes driven down in roughshod fashion, so dividends can be increased—"

"Now, now, just a minute, Greg"—Fletcher's face crimsoned angrily—"you know that is just not so. I won't hear such words. No road maintains higher standards than the T.N. & A.S. Our methods may at times appear severe, but competition demands it. We simply cannot allow any other road to get ahead of us. Why, you know yourself, if what you say is true, you'd not be under contract with us." He glared hotly at Quist.

Abruptly, Quist chuckled. "It's certainly easy to get under your skin, Jay. One word against the road and you're set to do murder."

That was almost true. The T.N. & A.S. was Jay Fletcher's "baby." His life was bound up in the company. In his position, that of Superintendent of Divisions, with the main office at El Paso, he had more to say in the operating of the railroad than many men bearing higher titles. He was unmarried and appeared to have no interest in life, aside from the company; his greatest

16

delight was seeing it grow strong and powerful. Most knotty problems concerning the operation of the road were dumped into Jay Fletcher's lap for solving, and on numerous occasions he had been forced to turn to Gregory Quist for aid.

"All right, all right," he said half sheepishly, relaxing under the geniality of Quist's smile. "Some day I'll learn, I hope, that you have to get a certain pleasure out of joshing me, before you'll consent to getting down to business." He drew out a couple of cigars and offered one to Quist. Quist refused, and Fletcher scratched a match to light his own weed, while Quist started to roll a brown-paper Bull Durham cigarette. Smoke lifted in the air to be caught up and swept away by the breeze through the open window. Fletcher said abruptly, "Greg, we're having a little trouble over on the Arizona Division. And it's nothing to do with murder this time, so you can rest easy."

"I've yet to see the day I rested easy on any job you handed me, Jay. Arizona, eh?" Quist's eyes narrowed thoughtfully. "Now I wonder—" He broke off. "What's the layout, Jay?"

"What do you know about the Arcanum country—Arcanum City?"

"I've passed through there a few times." Quist was smiling now. "On the train. All I know is hearsay. A lot of superstitious folks once called it the mystery country. That's years and years ago. Once the town was half wiped out by an Apache raid. It was just a small burg then, called Arcano. Lord, that took place half a century back. There was talk by superstitious folks about ghosts wandering in the mountains. All bosh of course."

"Probably," Fletcher conceded, "though that doesn't explain why thirty years back everybody in Arcano suddenly got up and departed from the town—just plain deserted it. Why? Where did they go?"

Quist raised the beer bottle to his lips, replaced it on his desk. "That's not hard to answer, Jay. I've talked to two or three old-timers who once lived there. There'd been some mining. That

17

petered out, and people had already begun to leave. The place was almost a ghost town when smallpox struck. That settled it, everybody got out, after burying their dead or taking the sick with them. There's no mystery about it, if you'll just talk to people who know, and ignore a lot of folks who like to spread wild tales. As a matter of fact, while the town was almost deserted, a number of cowmen had come in. Gradually the town began to grow again. Somebody named it Arcanum City. Today it is a right prosperous place."

"I hadn't heard all that before," Fletcher said thoughtfully. "At any rate, it's the present-day Arcanum City we have to deal with. Now I'd like you to go over there and—"

"No, Jay, it's not my kind of job."

"Wait, you don't even know what it is yet—"

"What's needed is a couple of good doctors. It's all out of my line."

"Now, look here, Greg, I haven't yet told you—"

"With two people dead, it's not my kind of work to determine which died first, Jay. You should know that. Hire a couple of medics."

Fletcher stared at him, eyes widening. "I'd almost swear you're a mind-reader, Greg. What do you know about this business?"

"Enough to realize I should keep out of it. I had a letter from a man named Bancroft. Apparently he has something to do with the hotel in Arcanum City. He stated that his sister had shot her husband, then killed herself. Both dead as doornails, I take it. And this Bancroft wanted to hire me to come there and for 'his peace of mind and that of the family,' determine which had died first, the man or the woman. I judge from the letter that the two turned into corpses within a minute or so of each other."

Fletcher nodded. "That's correct. Bancroft, eh? That would be Everett Bancroft, I imagine. I didn't meet him when I was there."

"You've been in Arcanum City, Jay?"

"Returned last week. I talked to our attorneys over there. They seemed stumped. One suggested I get you on the job. I'd already thought of that, and I agreed of course—"

"And everyone in town heard about that, I imagine," Quist said caustically.

Fletcher's cheeks reddened. "Why should you care, if you don't intend to go over there?" He didn't wait for a reply. "Have you written Bancroft yet?"

Quist nodded. "Haven't mailed the letter though. Told him I couldn't take the job because of my contract with the T.N. & A.S. And, Jay, I still can't see where I'd be any help over there."

"Bancroft didn't give you any details?"

"Said he'd furnish particulars if I came to Arcanum City."

"He didn't mention there was a great amount of money involved?"

Quist's eyes narrowed. "Is there? Maybe you'd best catch me up on the details, Jay."

Fletcher said mockingly, "I'm surprised to see you showing any interest, Greg. All right, here's the setup. Vance Callister owned the Box-VC Ranch over in that country. In addition to some mining interests he also owned the Callister Stage & Freight Company which operates a daily stage between Arcanum City and Wolverton, farther north. In short, he was a very wealthy man."

"Likely he also held a good block of T.N. & A.S. stock."

Fletcher smiled thinly. "Very likely, but that's not the reason I need your help—"

"And," Quist broke in, "the town of Wolverton is the terminus of the Rock Buttes Southern & Silverado Railroad. What's the connection, Jay?"

"First, Vance Callister is dead. We had planned to buy a right-of-way from him and build a road north to Wolverton. Our attorneys were a little dilatory in closing the deal and getting papers signed. Now, Callister is dead and we're up in the air. And there's no time to be lost."

"What's the rush?"

"I have it on good authority that the Rock Buttes Southern & Silverado are planning to build a road south. They want to buy the right-of-way we intend to get. If they can't get it, they'll go farther west—"

"Can't we go farther west too, if we want to build a line north?"

Fletcher shook his head. "The mountainous nature of the country doesn't make that feasible. Too expensive."

"But if the Rock Buttes outfit can afford—"

"We don't do business that way." Fletcher's lips tightened. "We always plan to operate at a profit. Rock Buttes & Silverado may be willing to lose money on such a project, but not the T.N. & A.S. Anyway, prestige demands we beat them on building a north-and-south line. Now there's just one logical, less expensive, route between Wolverton and Arcanum City, and that's through a stretch in the Arcanum Mountains known as Bisnaga Pass. We've got to have the right-of-way there."

"And Callister owned that?"

"His stage company owned the right-of-way straight through from Arcanum City to Wolverton. South of the pass, the route crosses Callister's Box-VC Ranch."

"I can't see where there is any particular problem, Jay. Even if Callister is dead, his heir or heirs certainly won't turn a deaf ear to the clink of good T.N. & A.S. money."

Fletcher eyed Quist with some scorn. "Yes. But that's just the rub. Who exactly is the heir? Callister's daughter or—?"

"Didn't he leave a will?"

"Yes"—shortly. "And that's just what complicates the business. Too much will, you might say."

"I'm waiting to hear."

Fletcher went on, "Callister has one daughter, Alexandra, whose mother died some years back. Callister married a second time, something about three months back, a woman named Anne Bancroft. Right after they married, a will was drawn up stating that if Vance Callister died first, all he owned, with the exception of a substantial sum of money to his daughter, Alexandra, and a few minor bequests, was to be inherited by his wife, Anne. Is that clear?"

"Clear as a fine brewing of good beer." Acting on his own hint, Quist tilted a bottle, emptied it and opened another bottle. He had begun to look interested.

Fletcher continued, "The same will—this will was signed by both Anne and Vance Callister, you understand?—provided that in the event Anne Callister died first, everything went to her husband, Vance Callister, including a twenty-thousand-dollar life insurance she insisted be taken out the day after they were married."

Quist's topaz eyes narrowed thoughtfully. "Maybe I commence to see complications. Still the lawyers should be able to—"

Fletcher snapped disgustedly, "You know how lawyers drag things out with their wrangling. We've got to have that right-of-way."

"As I see it there's just minor details to settle. I take it both Anne and Vance Callister received sudden-death wounds. But she'd have to be alive to kill him, before she committed suicide. Therefore, she must have lived the longer of the two. So her estate collects the money. Did she have any other relatives beside this Everett Bancroft?"

"A sister, Helen. Helen Bancroft operates the hotel in Arcanum City."

"And I suppose they're both interested. I still don't see why he wanted me to come there—"

"Just a minute, Greg. You haven't all the story yet. Nobody was at the ranch when Anne Callister killed her husband and then committed suicide—and nobody has an idea of what was back of the tragedy. Apparently they got on well—for all I heard they did, though you never know."

"When did this killing and suicide take place?"

"Just about a month back. As I say, nobody else was at the ranch when it happened. The ranch cook, a man named Hudson, returned from town that night and found the bodies. Naturally, he headed back to town for help as fast as a horse could carry him. The sheriff arrived with a doctor—" Fletcher broke off, then, "The sheriff hadn't been able to get Callister's regular doctor, but had brought an old broken-down sawbones named Iverson. This Doctor Iverson spends most of his time getting drunk and staying that way—"

Quist cut in sharply, "Why didn't they get the regular doctor?"

"He was out of town on a call at the time—at one of the ranches someplace. At any rate, sober or drunk, there wasn't anything any doctor could do for two dead people. Iverson made an examination before the inquest was held, of course—"

"The inquest didn't produce anything unusual?"

"Not a thing. The coroner's jury brought in a verdict that Anne Callister had killed her husband and then committed suicide. There was nothing else they could do. The gun was still in her hand when the sheriff arrived. It was Callister's six-shooter. His holster was empty. And so, the following day, the two bodies were buried. It was as simple as that—on the surface."

"What ruffled the surface?"

"The company lawyers were there, waiting for Callister to sign papers for the right-of-way. With Callister dead they began to worry, a little, but not too much. The will was read. As our lawyers interpreted things, Anne Callister, inasmuch as she had killed her husband, inherited the property, even though she also died almost immediately."

"In which case," Quist put in, "Anne Callister's sister and brother stood to inherit Anne's estate."

22

Fletcher nodded. "Exactly the way our attorneys saw the question, and they started to open negotiations with Helen and Everett Bancroft. The Bancrofts were willing to sell, of course. It looked just like a matter of drawing up proper papers. And then that damnable drunken Doctor Iverson upset the applecart—"

"In what way?"

"When he heard that the Bancrofts were due to inherit on the basis that Anne Callister had outlived her husband, he stated that according to his knowledge of the death wounds, there was a good chance, though both had died within a minute or so of each other, that Vance Callister could have been last to die."

"Jeepers! That would tangle things. Despite she was the one who killed him. Hmmm . . . By God, Jay! That's possible. And if so, the Bancrofts would be out of the running and Callister's daughter, Alexandra, would stand to inherit."

"Exactly what Alexandra's lawyer maintains. There's been a hell of a to-do about the business. The Bancrofts have a lawyer too. He's done his damnedest to get Iverson to change his remarks, but no go. The upshot of the matter is that the whole business is going to court to let a judge decide—maybe a jury too. Perhaps the bodies will have to be exhumed. I don't know and I don't care, which side wins, just as long as we can get that right-of-way. The big trouble arises in the fact that the case can't be heard until the fall session of court. And our company just can't wait that long. That's why I want you to go to Arcanum City—"

"But, Jay, I'm no medic—"

"No, blast it, but you can talk to both those doctors there. Perhaps you can dredge up something they've missed, or uncover something in some other way. You've done it before, Greg. Hell, man, won't you even try?" There was something pleading in Fletcher's tones. "Two people are dead of gunshots. You know guns and—"

"You're the boss, Jay. Why don't you just order me to go?"

"Because your contract states you don't have to take a job you don't want to, and I don't want to force you into anything. This is something I want you to be interested in—"

There came a knock on the door. Quist answered it and found the hotel clerk there, an envelope in his hand. "Is there a Mr. Fletcher with you, Mr. Quist?" Quist put out his hand. The man handed over the envelope with the single word, "Telegram."

Quist said "Thanks," and handed the envelope to Fletcher. Fletcher ripped open the envelope, quickly scanned it, a frown forming on his forehead.

Quist closed the door and reseated himself at the desk, lifting a beer bottle to his lips. He set down the bottle and looked inquiringly at Fletcher, catching the sudden exclamation that broke from the man. He said, "Anything wrong, Jay?"

Fletcher said slowly, "Somebody tried to murder Doctor Iverson last night."

"Tried to?"—sharply.

"The attempt wasn't successful. Didn't even hit him. This is from our attorney over there—what's up, Greg?"

Quist had moved quickly from his chair, slipped on his underarm holster and coat. He began packing extra shirts and other things into a brown leather satchel. He spoke while he moved about the room, "I'm heading for Arcanum City. There's skulduggery going on over there."

A look of relief passed across Fletcher's face. "Good, Greg. But there's no need of all this rush. Number Three isn't due for an hour yet. It will get you to Arcanum—"

"I'm not taking Number Three. But there's a train running east due at the depot—" Quist consulted his watch—"in just sixteen minutes. That will get me to Cannesville in time to catch the westbound Rock Buttes Limited—"

"Greg!" Fletcher looked aghast. "You wouldn't ride a competitor's train—?"

"In this case, yes," Quist snapped. "I want to get to Wolverton and catch the stage south to Arcanum City. It may take longer that way, but I figure it'll be safer. I'm not hankering to arrive by train—and I'd be expected that way—in Arcanum City, and find some sharpshooter stationed on a rooftop figuring to knock me off the instant I step from the train. By stagecoach I may be able to slip in unseen and get my bearings before any action starts. Remember you already hinted I'd be coming there."

Fletcher flushed uncomfortably. "Perhaps you're right, Greg. I should have kept my mouth shut. And feeling is running high in the town. Both Alexandra Callister and the Bancrofts have friends. People are beginning to take sides. Men who haven't a thing to win either way are making ugly talk about what will happen if their side loses. Both Alexandra Callister and Helen Bancroft are popular—"

"Lord!" Quist snapped shut his valise and shook his head. "Two women. One woman can cause enough dissension—but two—"

Fletcher said slyly, "Haven't I always heard you have a way with women, Greg?"

Quist swore. "I don't know what fool nonsense you've heard, Jay," he said shortly. Then, "You know damn' well I'm not concerned about those women. I'm just interested in whoever it was took a shot at that Doc Iverson."

"You think that has an important bearing on—?"

"Somebody was trying to shut the doc's mouth—kill off evidence. Drunk or not, it's damn' possible he knows what he's talking about. I want to learn who handled that gun—and why."

They shook hands. Now that Fletcher had shifted responsibility to Quist's capable shoulders, he appeared more relaxed. He said, "Good luck and be careful, Greg. You know you're lifting a big load from my mind. . . ."

The words trailed off to silence. Quist had already flung open the door and was headed down the hall, walking with quick even strides.

III

EARLY MORNING SUN poured down heat on Wolverton's frame depot, forcing the handful of the usual loungers back to the shadows beneath the overhanging roof. Far to the east the rails began to hum; a long-drawn whistle violated the peaceful air. A small boy darted out to the edge of the Rock Buttes Southern & Silverado depot platform and squinted against the sun and along the quivering tracks.

"Here she comes!" he screeched.

A station attendant pushed out on the platform, watch in hand and peered toward the rapidly approaching train. "Six twenty-nine and a half," he announced to no one in particular. "The Limited's on time, as always."

Like some great puffing monster the powerful locomotive swept up to the station and on past. Black clouds of smoke and white steam swirled around the loungers who drew back in some awe. Cinders showered down. Brakes sounded shrilly to the clanking of the panting monster up ahead. The train ground to a stop; passengers began to disgorge from the coaches. Quist was one of the first to alight, carrying his small valise. Removing his flat-topped sombrero, he whipped it against one corduroyed leg to remove the dust of travel, then replaced it, tilted slightly, on his shock of tawny hair.

He moved on through the depot and to the street beyond. Wolverton's main street stretched east and west before his eyes, a typical frontier-day town: adobe and frame buildings, false-fronts; the usual saloons. Pedestrians passed along the sidewalks.

A smile twitched Quist's lips as he turned left. "Likely it would break Jay's heart," he mused, "if I told him the Rock Buttes furnished good service. Probably he realizes that, though. That's why he's so anxious to secure that right-of-way. Well, competi-

26

tion is the heart of progress, they say. I just hope I don't find too much competition in Arcanum City. Me, I'd like to progress a few years yet."

A block east he saw the sign: Callister Stage & Freight Co., in faded, sun-blistered paint. Beneath, stood the wide entrance. Quist entered. A clerk stood at a high flat-topped desk, beside which was a weighing scales. Several people stood about, baggage at their feet, while the clerk argued with a fat woman whose trunk stood on the scales.

"Sorry, madam," the clerk was saying, "you don't understand. It's the *trunk* we're charging extra for. Excess weight."

Quist sauntered across the room to read a yellowed, fly-specked poster on one wall, giving particulars regarding coach fares:

CALLISTER STAGE & FREIGHT COMPANY

DAILY TRIPS MADE BETWEEN ARCANUM CITY AND WOLVERTON.

Utmost Speed and Safety Provided in Modern Concord Coaches.

Equipped with Latest Improvements

NORTH BOUND: Monday, Wednesday, Friday.
SOUTH BOUND: Tuesday, Thursday, Saturday.

No Passage Sold For Sundays.

| | Tariff of Fares Between Points | |
	South Bound	North Bound
Wolverton	———	$10.20
Horse Shoe Tanks	$ 1.95	8.25
Pancake Flat	3.45	6.75
Ocotillo Mound	4.80	5.40
Black Ore Springs	6.00	4.20
Wood's Digging's	7.05	3.15
Honey-Pod Ranch	7.95	2.25
Bisnaga Creek	8.85	1.35
Arcanum City	10.20	———
	Round Trip	$18.00

Stops made at Intermediate Points by Special Request.

Passengers traveling with Excess of 20 Lbs. Baggage, excluding Guns, Will Be Charged for same at Tariff of 10c Per Lb.

Dinner served Gratis of Charge at Black Ore Tanks to all passengers traveling Entire Length of Route.

Coaches leave Promptly at 7:00 a.m. and Arrive with Due Diligence & Dispatch.

Vance Callister, Sole Prop.

The argument with the fat woman came to an end. Quist moved back to the desk. The clerk asked, "Where to, mister?"

"Arcanum City."

Quist's valise was lifted and dropped on the scales. "No excess," the clerk stated. "You want a round trip?"

"One way."

The clerk grinned. "Don't you expect to come back?"

"About that," Quist replied, something grim in his tones, "I'm not sure yet."

The clerk eyed him sharply for a moment, then shrugged and scribbled some notations on a pad of paper, which he tore off and handed to Quist. "That'll be ten bucks twenty, mister." And when Quist had paid him and received change from a twenty-dollar gold piece, "Have a good trip. Coach leaves at seven. Prompt."

"Have I got time to grab a cup of coffee?"

"Depends on how fast you drink it, mister. I said seven prompt."

By the time Quist had returned from a small restaurant, half a block down the street, the coach with its six horses was waiting before the doorway of the stage office. The driver, a middle-aged man, in dusty denims, wide hat and vest, was busily engaged in stowing away baggage in the stage boots, front and rear. Five seats in the coach were already taken, one by the fat woman whose trunk had been lashed on top, so Quist quickly climbed in

28

to take his place. Two men glanced within the coach, then disappointedly climbed to the roof, where they seated themselves, legs dangling over the edge.

The clerk emerged with the strongbox, said something to the driver and went back to his office. The strongbox was boosted to the top. A small crowd had gathered to witness the departure of the stage. One of them yelled at the driver, "How 'bout it, Buzzard, figurin' to make a record drive this time?"

Buzzard Greer spat tobacco juice. "I allus makes record time, squirt." He raised his voice above the laughter, "Come on, folks! Who's for Arcanum City and way points. Get a move on if you're goin' with me. Ain't no time to pick daisies now."

A Mexican woman enveloped in a long flowing dress and with a *serape* over her head, emerged from the stage office, a live chicken, tied by the feet, in one hand. The chicken, head down, squawked miserably. The woman peered into the interior of the coach, saw all seats were taken.

"Better shake yer dew-claws and tootsies, señora," the driver urged, "if you're ridin' with us."

Laughter from the assembled onlookers. The Mexican woman looked helplessly toward the top of the coach. The chicken squawked. There ensued more laughter.

Quist stepped out of the coach, took the woman's arm and helped her into his seat. A voluble torrent of Spanish engulfed him. *"Gracias, señor, gracias!"*

"Por nada," Quist returned courteously, touching one hand to the brim of his sombrero. He turned and climbed to the top, seated himself cross-legged.

The driver addressed the loungers. "We got one of them Galahads with us this mawnin', gents."

A flurry of cheers greeted the remark. Quist laughed and rolled and lighted a cigarette. The clerk again emerged from his office. "Seven o'clock, Buzzard. Time to be fanning that breeze."

The driver's watch was already in his hand. "Damn! Don't I know it. I'm waiting for Charley."

The clerk swore. "That guard late again? I'll see if I can find him for you." Somebody in the crowd mentioned having seen the shotgun-guard in the Beehive Saloon, and the clerk started off down the street, moving with angry strides. The driver mounted to his seat.

Quist swung around on top of the coach, gaze following the clerk, saw him enter a barroom. Within a few minutes he emerged with a sullen-looking individual carrying a sawed-off double-barreled shotgun. The man arrived, jerked his sombrero low on his forehead and climbed to the seat beside the driver. Angry remarks passed between the two men.

The guard raised his voice: "Hell, Buzzard, what difference does a coupla minutes make?"

"I got a skeedule to maintain—"

"Aw, you can make up the time easy—"

"And kill my hawsses, I s'pose?"

"That's up to you. I'm sick of this job anyway—"

The clerk's voice cut coldly in, "Is this stage goin' to leave to-day, or ain't it?"

"It's leavin'. *Pronto!*" the driver stated curtly. He kicked off the brake, reached for his long whip, gathered reins in his hands. "Here we go, folks! Hang on to yer hats!"

The long whip sailed out, snapped viciously above the horses' heads. The coach lurched into sudden action; the passengers' heads jerked back and those on top grabbed at the metal railing that ran around the roof of the vehicle.

Straight down the center of the street the horses tore, made a sharp turn along a road that led to open country. Buzzard Greer's long whip cracked again. The six horses straightened out, threw their combined weights against the harness. Dust rose in billowing clouds at the rear of the stage as the horses increased pace.

Quist drew the bandanna at his throat up around his mouth and nose, jerked his sombrero lower on his head. Wind whipped into his face, carrying small particles of dust and tiny bits of gravel. The stage rolled on, the body swaying on its thorough braces, through a swiftly moving kaleidoscope of alkali waste, mesquite and sage. Ahead, low hills climbed toward the mountains, their peaks etched against the cobalt, cloudless sky.

One of the men on the roof said something to Quist about the country through which they were passing. Quist nodded, smiled shortly but made no effort to maintain a conversation. There was little cracking of the driver's whip now. It wasn't necessary. Occasionally, the coach slowed momentarily as the driver tooled his spans around a chuckhole in the road, or deftly swung them aside where the road elbowed around an outcropping of upthrust granite. Neither he nor the guard were speaking to each other, so far as Quist could determine. The guard sat slumped in his seat, hat low on forehead. Now and then Buzzard gave the man a brief glance in which disgust, anger, showed plain.

Quist considered the matter. Stage drivers, and shotgun guards as well, took a certain pride in their jobs, particularly in seeing that a stage departed on the time advertised. Stages were sometimes late in departing, true, but Quist could never remember a time when it had been the fault of the driver or guard. Generally it was some passenger responsible for a tardy take-off. Nor were guards known to be somewhat under the weather from drink when they left.

Quist hadn't missed the guard's slight stagger when he emerged from the saloon, or the somewhat uncertain grasp on the rail as he clambered up to his seat. Quist studied the man. A sort of sullen brute, he decided, and not the type generally found working on reliable stage routes. Perhaps there was more to this matter than met the eye. He wondered what the passengers inside the coach were like; he'd not been seated long enough to size

31

them up. That's something that I'll have to take care of at the first opportunity, he mused.

He gave his attention to the road ahead, where it stretched in an ever-diminishing ribbon between vast seas of mesquite, cactus and sage. There were more hills to be seen now, and far ahead he could see rocky foothills climbing up and up to the Arcanum Mountains. An occasional jackrabbit was seen scurrying frantically away from the road, and once a coyote went coursing with swift strides through the brush. One of the men on top of the coach drew his six-shooter and emptied it in the direction of the coyote, but the animal kept going and disappeared in a patch of underbrush.

The man reloaded his six-shooter, swearing disgruntledly. "Had I been standing still I'd hit that varmint," he yelled through the rush of wind at Quist.

"Likely." Quist nodded and withdrew to silence.

They had reached the first stop, Horse Shoe Tanks, almost before Quist realized it. Horse Shoe Tanks had little to offer except a change of horses. It was typical of the small stations on stage routes: just a few buildings thrown up and a couple of corrals. Farther to the west a handful of adobe shacks showed above the sea of sage and mesquite.

Six fresh horses were already waiting when the stage pulled to a halt. Buzzard Greer leaped down and helped unharness his panting horses, while he and the attendant worked feverishly to get the new spans into traces. The shotgun guard sat on his seat without moving. Here, the Mexican woman with the chicken left the stage and after again thanking Quist, started to trudge off through the cactus and sage in the direction of the adobe shacks, the chicken still squawking.

Quist dropped down from the top of the coach and resumed his seat within, the leather cushion being hot to the touch. One or two passengers had dismounted to stretch their legs, but hurriedly got back again. There was small time lost changing horses. Within another minute the stage had again lurched into movement, to the accompaniment of sharp whip-cracking by the driver.

Now that railroads were reaching farther and farther through the West, stages endeavored to meet such competition with speedy journeys. Quist glanced at his watch. It wasn't yet a quarter to nine and already some thirteen-odd miles had passed to the rear.

His seat faced toward the back of the coach. Across from him sat the big fat woman who had argued with the clerk regarding her trunk. Wedged into the same seat were a pair of what Quist termed "ladies of the night." They wore plumed hats and frilly dresses. Their faces were now as red as the rouge on their cheeks; they looked decidedly uncomfortable. Listening to their conversation, Quist learned they were headed for Black Ore Springs, "a lively growing town," and that they'd been to Wolverton on a shopping trip. One was brunette; the other a peroxide blonde. The fat woman had by this time fallen asleep, her weight sagging against the blonde. From time to time the girl made a futile effort to straighten up the weighty bulk, but there was too much poundage to budge.

On Quist's seat rode two drummers, one a whisky salesman, the other dealing in mining machinery. Conversation eventually brought out the fact they also were traveling to Black Ore Springs. They had made a few joshing remarks to the painted beauties across from them, but the girls were too uncomfortable to cooperate at present.

At Pancake Flat, ten miles farther on, the next change of horses was effected, and one of the men on top left the stage. Here there were a few buildings set in an unusually flat stretch of decomposed granite wasteland, with stunted sage growing sparsely from the sandy particles glistening brightly under the hot sun. Again the coach lurched on its way.

Hot wind and dust flowed through the open windows of the coach. Alkali settled on passengers and clogged throats and nostrils. The fat woman snored on, perspiring profusely and seeming to give off a certain heat of her own. One of the ladies fanned herself ceaselessly with a lace handkerchief that sent forth a sweetish aroma of Jockey Club perfume. She smiled wistfully at Quist, "It's mighty warm, sir."

"Certainly is," he nodded.

"You going to Black Ore Springs?" she asked.

Quist just shook his head, then added, "Farther."

The brunette got into the conversation. "We thought maybe you was the new faro dealer who was hired for the Fan-Tan House."

Quist smiled and said no. The whisky salesman asked the brunette, "Fan-Tan House opening again? I thought after that last killing the law would close 'em for good."

"What's one killing out here in the West, more or less?" the mining machinery salesman cut in. "Things go on the same and always will."

"No, siree," his companion denied. "Things is getting settled. The West ain't what it used to be. The law has seen to that. You take just one good gunfighter, pin a badge on him, and he'll clean up any tough town you care to name—just like, for instance, Wyatt Earp did in Tombstone a few years back."

"Wonder if there was any truth in that rumor Earp wore a bulletproof vest," the other man said.

"Never heard that he did. I wonder was he as fast with his gun as Bill Hickok or Billy Bonney."

"Billy the Kid wasn't ever a peace officer."

"He could shoot like hell, though."

"The West is full of men with a fast gun," the machinery sales-man stated. "For instance there was that piece in *Karper's Weekly* that told about a feller named Quist, a railroad detective. He's getting quite a rep." He appealed to Quist: "You ever run across him, mister?"

Quist frowned thoughtfully. "Seems like I've heard of him, someplace. Yeah, I read that piece. Sounded full of buffalo chips to me. These writers—"

"Don't think much of Quist, eh? How do you figure he'd stack up against a gunsharp like, say, Hickok, if they tangled?"

"Hickok being dead, I can't say. Alive, he'd like's not shoot Quist's block off."

The coach rocked on. Quist put his head back, closed his eyes and pretended to sleep, listening in some amusement to the talk of the two salesmen. The whisky salesman said, "Best man with a gun I ever saw was up in Kansas City one time. He was travel-ing with Texas Jack's Wild West Show and Exhibition. Feller named Jamison. Used a forty-four Winchester and broke glass balls. And it was loaded with a regular cartridge too. Not just scatter shot like most of these sharpshooters use. He was right good with a six-shooter too. Used a mirror and shot over his shoulder at bottles. Smashed every one of 'em. Hot-tempered cuss though. I heard later he killed a man for fussin' with his wife, and went to the pen for it. . . ."

Quist, eyes still closed, thought idly it was unusual for a sharp-shooter to use a forty-four. His own favorite caliber. Never heard of anyone named Jamison that he could remember. Still, gun-men were plentiful.

The coach rattled across a plank bridge over a dry wash. Quist opened his eyes and sat up. He heard Buzzard Greer bawl "Oco-tillo Mound," as the coach stopped. Fresh horses waited; harness jangled. Ocotillo Mound boasted a small saloon, and the two sales-men hurriedly dismounted to grab a quick "snort." The remain-

35

ing passenger atop the coach got down, and Buzzard got his valise from the boot. The fat woman snored on.

Looking at his watch, Quist saw it was eleven-thirty. He glanced from the window. The mountains seemed nearer now. Back of the town rose a low hill covered with ocotillo—devil's riding whip, some called it—already beginning to push forth its scarlet tips. Here and there, organ cactus climbed the hillsides.

The salesmen emerged from the saloon, wiping mouths, and resumed their seats. Buzzard's side of the coach sagged as he climbed aloft. The whip cracked and the stage again got under way. Both girls were fanning themselves with handkerchiefs now, and the coach was redolent of perfume. The country flowed past in a continual dusty scene.

IV

BY THIS TIME one of the girls had fallen asleep; she and the snoring fat woman appeared to be propping each other up. The other girl passed a couple of small cards to the salesmen, glanced at Quist and vetoed the idea. Less than two hours later, Buzzard Greer tooled his sweat- and alkali-streaked horses into Black Ore Springs station, which owed its existence to the Red Windmill mine situated back in the hills. Nearer to the town were a stamp mill and smelting plant, its stacks sending out a thick brassy smoke that permeated the air with a thick haze. A street of sorts pushed up toward the mine and there were other cross streets, crowded with adobe and frame buildings.

Buzzard Greer was calling, "All out for Black Ore Springs! Half-hour layover for dinner. All out!" He came around to the side of the coach, reached through the window and shook the fat woman awake. "Here's your stop, missus. I'll have your trunk down in a minute."

Two attendants were unharnessing while Buzzard worked at the trunk and lowered it to the earth at the end of a rope. He dropped down again, opened the boots. The brunette was already getting out on the opposite side with a "Home again, thank Gawd!" The blonde was close on her heels, shaking out her skirts. Quist dismounted, followed by the two salesmen. The three made their way into the stage station, where dinner was being served in a room with whitewashed adobe walls.

Quist found a table alone and a waiter almost immediately slammed down in front of him a platter of leathery steak and fried potatoes, without waiting for him to order. Coffee and a triangle of dried apple pie next appeared. Some muddy-looking water was splashed into a glass, and the waiter headed for another table.

A doorway in the dining room opened into a barroom next door, whence came loud voices and the clinking of glasses. Quist's nose twitched at the beery smell from the barroom, and he started to eat his dinner. People passed in and out of the room. In a short time the tables were all full.

A tall girl rose from a table in one corner—she looked at least six feet—then reached for her black sombrero and jammed it down tightly on a wealth of shining auburn hair, done neatly in a knob at her nape, tucking in a few stray wisps here and there, until the hat felt secure. She picked up a short leather jacket and tossed it over one arm. Quist had barely noticed the girl when he first came in; now he eyed her with interest. She was, he concluded, "a darn good-looking woman, with all the curves in the right places. Pretty nice curves too." A mite tall, perhaps, but that was a minor discrepancy when a man considered those long-lashed gray eyes, the fine straight nose and the full lips. A lot of determination in the chin, too, denoting some considerable strength of will.

She wore a mannish flannel shirt, properly filled, with a blue

37

bandanna knotted at the open throat. A corduroy divided riding skirt and black leather riding boots completed the costume. Her stride, when she started for the doorway, was long and even-paced; her back ramrod straight. Admiring eyes followed the girl as she crossed the dining room.

Buzzard Greer met her as he was entering the doorway. He executed a mock bow. "The carriage awaits, muh lady."

The girl gave him a cool smile. "Have a good trip, Buzzard?"

"Never had a bad one, Alex. Cut three minutes off my time, even with a late start. Let's see if you can make Arcanum in as good time, and that's the shortest stretch of the trip. But I'm glad to be done for the day. It's hot on top that coach—"

"What's this about a late start?" the girl cut in abruptly.

"Charley again," Buzzard explained. "Must be it's glue he gets at that Beehive Saloon in Wolverton. He just can't seem to tear loose from the stuff when I'm ready to start—"

"Where is he now?"

Buzzard Greer shrugged. "I ain't seen him since he got off his seat when we got here—first move he'd made since we started. Sulky as a kid. I tried to talk to him. He didn't take it kindly."

The girl nodded thoughtfully, and passed on through the door. Buzzard came on in and sought a place at a table. Quist rolled and lighted a cigarette, then made his way to the bar. Here a bottle of beer washed some of the dust from his throat. He glanced at his watch. Five minutes to one. He considered having a second beer, then passed up the idea. The coach would be starting shortly. Leaving the saloon he stepped out to the long-roofed gallery that fronted the dining room, saloon and stage station. It was unbelievably cool on the shadowed gallery, though the sun blazed down beyond.

At one end of the gallery the girl stood talking to Buzzard Greer. He heard her say, "I've no idea where he's gone. The clerk in the station said he left word he was sick and wouldn't continue the trip. That's a fine way—" Her voice sounded wrathful.

Buzzard cut in. "Doesn't sound very sick to me. Blackie White said he saw him mounting a hawss out back of the station, right after we got in. Reckon he's just sore and aimed to quit. 'Fraid to face—"

"That's neither here nor there," the girl snapped, "the coach can't leave without a guard—"

"Oh, cripes," Buzzard said, "it won't hurt nothing to go 'thout one. There ain't no money in the strongbox—just a small sack of U.S. mail."

"The law demands a shotgun guard on every trip, Buzzard. I'm not figuring to break the law. That's definite. Well, we'll just have to see what we can do."

The pair talked a minute longer, then disappeared around the corner of the building.

Quist considered the question. Apparently the coach was to be late in departing, owing to the absence of the shotgun guard, and there would have been time for that second beer anyway. Turning the thought to action, Quist stepped back into the saloon and ordered a bottle of beer. But he didn't stay at the bar long. Taking the bottle with him, he moved back to the shaded gallery to wait.

By this time fresh horses had been harnessed, but there was no sign of a driver or guard. Quist frowned. What did the girl—Alex, Buzzard had called her—have to do with the stage? Alex? Alex? ... The name struck a responsive chord in Quist's memory. Then the thought occurred to him: Vance Callister had had a daughter named Alexandra. Could this tall girl be the daughter? It was possible. What was she, station manager at Black Ore Springs, or something of the sort?

And why had Charley, the shotgun guard, disappeared so abruptly? Something was funny about the situation. Quist glanced again at the coach, and saw that a fresh passenger had been picked up at this stop. From what Quist could see of him, he was an ugly-visaged individual, with a week's growth of beard on his leathery face. Apparently the man was growing impatient at the delay; one hand drummed impetuously on the edge of the coach window, and every so often he scowled toward the stage station. There didn't appear to be any other passengers, except this man and Quist, from this point on.

Buzzard Greer came hurrying past, frowning, talking to himself. Quist said, "Stage is going to be late leaving, isn't it, driver?"

Buzzard stopped short. "Yeah, but I won't be driving. My drive ends at Black Ore Springs." He started on.

Quist caught his arm. "What's the delay?"

"Ain't got no shotgun guard. Charley plumb up and quit on us. Alex and me is trying to hire somebody else—"

"Alex?"

"Miss Callister. She's—"

"Vance Callister's daughter?"

"Yeah. You know her? Vance is dead—"

"I've heard of her. What are you going to do if you can't get a guard?"

"You tell me and I'll tell you," Buzzard grumbled.

"Got a driver, all right, I suppose?"

"Yeah. Alex—"

"Hey, Buzzard," interrupted the impatient passenger in the coach, "is this broken-down freight-cart intendin' to leave today?"

Buzzard's features clouded up as he glanced out toward the stage. "It shouldn't make much difference to you if it don't, Yoakum. If you ain't satisfied, go get your money back." He added in an aside to Quist, "That damn' no-good. Don't know where he ever got enough money to get to Wood's Diggin's. The town must have paid him to get out. Well, I gotta keep tryin' to find a guard."

He brushed on past. Quist noted that the passenger in the coach had made no reply to Buzzard Greer, beyond a nasty look of hate. Quist finished his beer, set the bottle down against the wall. When he straightened up, he saw that the girl had again appeared at the far end of the gallery. He moved along to approach her, touched fingers to the edge of his sombrero and said, "I understand you're having trouble getting a guard for the rest of the trip."

"That's right," she said curtly. "You in a hurry to be on your way, mister?"

Quist smiled and quoted from the placard he'd read in Wolverton: "'Coaches leave promptly . . .'" He was still smiling, thinking she was even better looking than he'd at first decided. "It's a matter of convenience, rather than haste, convenience to you—"

"It's damned inconvenient to me," she snapped, then relaxed, taking in his topaz eyes and the way his lips curved. She started an explanation, "My shotgun guard has quit, and we can't seem to find anyone to take the job on such short notice. Well, I guess Buzzard will just have to drive the rest of the trip and I'll—but I hate to ask him—"

"What's the job pay, ma'am?" Quist asked, trying to make his tones sound humble and not quite succeeding.

She eyed him narrowly a moment then, tersely, "If it's of any interest to you, twenty dollars for the rest of the trip." Spying Greer a few rods away, she started toward him.

Quist took a step to block her way. "You've hired a shotgun guard, Miss Callister."

The girl stiffened, looked him over from head to foot, and frowned, "I don't know. You're a stranger to me. You ever done any shotgun riding?"

"No, ma'am, but I've handled shotguns once or twice."

A look of exasperation crossed Alexandra Callister's face. "Most men in this country have," she snapped, "but that doesn't necessarily mean—"

Buzzard Greer's voice interrupted, "Danged if I can find one hombre to take the job, Alex. They all got work to do or they can't be away that long or—"

"This gentleman has offered to take the job, Buzzard," she interrupted. "What do you think?"

"As a convenience to the stage company, only," Quist said gravely. "And for the twenty dollars, of course. And I'd expect a rebate on my fare. After all, I had to pay for the trip and if I have to work too—"

"You'd get your money—and the rebate," the girl stated shortly, "but—"

"Cripes, why not, Alex?" Buzzard put in. He seemed a trifle surprised at Quist's offer, but fell in with the idea.

"But we know nothing about him—"

"Perhaps," Quist interposed, "if I proved trustworthy today, you'd consider me for a steady job, Miss Callister."

"He's real perlite to ladies," Buzzard put in, and added how Quist had given up his seat to the Mexican woman with the chicken.

"Shotgun guarding is no place for parlor manners," Alex Callister stated crisply. She looked again at Quist and caught something like a twinkle in his yellow eyes. For some reason it reassured her. "Moses on the mountain! Why not?" she came to an abrupt decision. "All right, you're hired, mister. What's your name?"

"Gregory, ma'am."

"You're ready to leave now, Gregory?"

"Just waiting for the coach to start. If you'll trot out your driver we can—"

"I'll be doing the driving," Alex Callister stated shortly.

Quist's jaw dropped. "You? You—the driver?"

The girl's gray eyes narrowed. "You afraid to ride with me?"

"Er—no—that is—"

"Get up on that seat, then, mister. I promise not to spill you off."

42

"You'll be safe, Gregory," Buzzard said, grinning. "She's a pretty good driver." And added depreciatingly, "For a woman."

Quist didn't catch the girl's reply, only the furious tone, as he started in the direction of the stage. Then he heard Buzzard's taunting ". . . and don't wear out that whip, tryin' to show off, Alex. Treat our new guard gentle-like and brake on the curves. . . ."

Quist had reached the stage. He opened the door and reached in for his satchel. The lone passenger gave him a sneering glance. "Got a job, huh, feller?"

Quist said quietly, "There's nothing wrong with your ears, anyway. Too bad the rest of your carcass doesn't catch up."

The man bridled. "You hintin' there's something wrong with the rest of me?"

Quist said, "No—I wasn't *hinting*."

"Why—damn your hide—" The man grasped the edge of the doorway, prepared to get out.

Quist got his satchel, stepped back and slammed the door. The man just jerked his hand back in time to avoid a set of crushed fingers. "You ought to watch these doors," Quist said pleasantly, "these late-model Concords fit tight."

He moved around the coach, tossed his satchel to the top, and climbed up, just as Alex Callister was mounting on the opposite side. A few men had gathered to watch the departure and a cheer went up as the girl skillfully grouped the reins in her fingers, cracked the whip and started the horses into running motion.

Quist sat at her side, shotgun cradled between his legs, admiring the deft ease with which Alexandra Callister handled her spans. The whip rarely came into use; now and then she flicked the off-swing horse lightly. Once she said something in a low tone about its being "a lazy beast."

They rode in silence, the way gradually mounting to higher terrain as they passed through rolling foothills, dotted with outcroppings of sandstone of a deep gray color, which grew darker

43

as the stage advanced, until at places it was almost black. The mountains ahead were the same somber color.

The rush of wind past the coach made talking in a normal voice almost impossible, that and the thudding of hoofs and rattle of harness. Anyway, the girl didn't appear inclined for conversation. From time to time Quist glanced sidewise at her; her features seemed set in tight lines as though she were trying to solve some deep problem.

Small sandy particles worked into Quist's mouth. His teeth gritted on them. It wasn't pleasant, but he realized the girl was putting up with the same inconvenience, and his admiration for her lifted another notch. Again he had drawn his bandanna up across his nose and mouth, and in a few minutes saw the girl do likewise. Now only her gray eyes showed above the blue bandanna and the sombrero was jammed tightly down on her head.

Quist had already examined the shotgun and found it ready loaded. He wondered what he would do if more shells were required some place along the trip. As though realizing what was passing through his mind, the girl called through the rush of wind, "You'll find more loads in that small drawer under the seat, Gregory." He nodded, and after a minute she asked, "Don't you carry a six-shooter?"

He reached behind him, lifted his satchel, dropped it again. Words weren't needed, and it had saved an explanation about his underarm holster, beneath his coat. More silence and more miles of rocks and sand and cactus flowed past.

It was three o'clock in the afternoon when the girl pulled her panting horses to a stop at Wood's Diggings, a small mining settlement composed of one general store, two saloons and various buildings running all the way from small adobe and stone shacks to adobe walls with sheets of corrugated-iron forming roofs. The stage station was whitewashed and looked neat. Two men brought out horses and the exchange of spans was quickly made.

44

The girl dropped lightly down from the coach, said something to one of the attendants. He glanced up at Quist a moment then went on with his work. Quist guessed she was asking if either of the attendants knew him. The passenger named Yoakum dismounted and left the door standing open as he started for the saloon. He glanced back once, defiantly, at Quist, then went on. Quist climbed down and closed the door, regained his seat.

The girl mounted, again gathered the reins. The attendants yelled their good-byes and were replied to with a slight raising of the girl's whip which again cracked the horses into action. Quist said, "I take it that passenger wasn't going any farther."

"Who, Yoakum? No. His ticket just called for Woods Diggings." She added, "I never before knew him to ride the stage."

"Who is he?"

The girl shrugged. "Just one of the hangers-on around Black Ore Tanks. Never holds a job long. Too quarrelsome. Just a lazy loafer, I guess. I've never yet heard anyone have a good word for him." She hesitated. "It could be I owe you an apology. I was a mite short about taking you on, back there in Black Ore Springs—"

Quist broke in to tell her to forget it. From then on the girl was more talkative. Talking came easier now that they weren't making such fast time. The way continually grew more rocky. At times the coach passed through narrow roads blasted from solid black rock, the sides rising steeply at either side. The flat country had been left far behind now, as the coach wended its way deeper through the mountains. There were more curves in the route as the road took advantage of lower levels wherever offered. Cactus and mesquite were still to be seen, but the growth was nowhere near so plentiful as during the earlier stages of the journey. Now the Arcanum Mountains seemed almost to tower over head. A harsh-looking country, Quist mused, only half listening to the girl as her voice came through the rushing windflow.

". . . and after we get through Bisnaga Pass," she was saying, "and reach Honey-Pod Ranch, the route flattens out again and we'll make better speed. My stretch is the shorter of the two on the route, but nobody makes the time Buzzard Greer does on his half. It's really good you came along as guard. Otherwise, I'd have had to ask Buzzard, and he's already done double duty a couple of days. You see, the regular driver on this stretch broke his leg, and I couldn't get a new man until tomorrow, so I've been doing the driving the last three days." She laughed suddenly. "Feel better about traveling with a woman driver by this time, Gregory?"

Quist grinned a trifle sheepishly. "If I was as certain about my shotgun-guarding as I am about your driving, everything would be hunky-dory, Miss Callister. But you must admit it's an unusual job for a woman."

"Probably," she conceded. "On the other hand, stagecoach history tells of several women drivers. There was quite a famous one in the early days of New England. And the Birch lines, out in California, employed one until she died, some years back. Her name, I think, was Charlotte Pankhurst, though they didn't learn until she died she was a woman."

"You certainly handle those ribbons well," Quist complimented.

"Thanks. I should know how. When I was younger I used to sneak away from the ranch and go out with the drivers. They taught me. My father—he owns—owned—the line you know—he was furious when he learned what I'd been doing. Said it was no way for a lady to behave. He got over it though. From time to time since, I've driven stage, when we were a driver short. Ever handle six horses?"

"Once or twice"—cautiously. "A long while back."

"Let's see what you can do, Gregory. If we hire you regularly, this is a good time to learn your capabilities."

They made an exchange of seats with scarcely any slowing of

46

the swaying coach. Quist distributed the reins between his fingers, and settled to the business at hand. As though sensing a new hand at the ribbons, the horses started to slow. Quist sent the whip in a vicious snapping above the horses' backs, and they immediately picked up speed again. The girl leaned back, holding the shotgun.

The stage rolled easily on. Quist glanced at the girl, smiling thinly. "All right?"

"You're expert," she exclaimed.

"Not quite. It's been a long time. I can see already my finger muscles would tire before many miles."

"They'd regain condition. Mister Gregory, you're hired if you want the job."

"We'll talk it over at the end of the line," Quist laughed.

He gave himself over to the business of tooling the spans, finding a certain enjoyment in driving the coach. His wrists became a bit cramped and he relaxed a trifle the grip on the reins. Then it came easier.

They weren't making such good time now, however, though it had nothing to do with the driving. There were more curves in the road, necessitating considerable braking. Rock shoulders rose on either side. Slopes lifted, hilly and boulder-strewn, on either hand. Glancing ahead, Quist thought he saw a break in the mountains.

"Bisnaga Pass?" he asked the girl.

Alex Callister nodded. "We'll start to drop momentarily just around the next curve. The country opens up a trifle . . ."

Quist didn't catch her following words. He was inent on reining the horses around the bend. Jagged sandstone bordered the way. Then he was safely around the turn and the slopes on either side flattened momentarily. Now there wasn't more than a five-foot shoulder of loose earth and rock at either side, and from this shoulder the land rose at a slight incline to form hilly slopes, strewn with cactus, stunted mesquite and granite boulders which had been tumbled from greater heights.

Quist's gaze scanned the slopes, thinking what a fine place this would make for an ambush. He stiffened suddenly as his gaze caught a momentary glimpse of a metallic glitter reflecting the afternoon sunlight. Then the brief gleam was gone and he gave his attention to the next curve where the road dipped. That was negotiated with ease. Then came the girl's sudden exclamation, something about a landslide. Quist swore abruptly and snapped, "That's no landslide, girl."

Not fifty yards ahead on the road, the way was barred by a tumbled heap of boulders and brush. Not huge boulders it is true, but the jumble of rock was large enough to delay the coach for some minutes while it was being removed.

"Hang on to your hat!" Quist yelled. "We're not stopping!"

V

HIS WHIP sailed out with a vicious report. The horses lunged ahead. Quist switched the reins, bunching them in his left hand while his right swept to the underarm holster. The six-shooter flashed out, swung toward the rock-tumbled slope on the right. The five detonations seemed almost to blend into one as leaden slugs sprayed a wide arc above the point where the roadway was blocked.

"Use that shotgun, damn it!" he shouted through the rush of wind. He shoved the empty forty-four back into holster, again distributed reins among the proper fingers. The roadblock was closer now. From the slope above came the crack of a repeating rifle and the explosions of six-shooters. Then the girl got the shotgun into play. There were two heavy *pows!* But now Quist paid attention to none of the shooting.

Abruptly he swung the galloping leaders toward the side of the five-foot sloping shoulder of road. There was a moment's hesitation, then the horses recognized the hands of a master on the reins and promptly obeyed. There were more shots flying wild from the hillside, but the coach wasn't making a good target.

Up, up it rocked, careening insanely as the wheels struck the slope. For a brief moment Quist thought the vehicle would topple, but the horses, hoofs scrabbling on stony soil, surged furiously ahead. There was a final lunge and they'd reached relatively level going, above the road and running parallel to it, the coach bounding violently on loose rocks. Once it lurched sickeningly to one side, a wheel spinning madly, until once more the stage settled back on an even keel. The animals plunged on, the stage rocking crazily. Rocks loomed ahead, but always by some miracle Quist managed to get past them, braking at the right time and swinging his leaders in the right direction.

And then they were past the barrier in the road. The girl was on her knees fumbling with fresh shotgun shells. Quist didn't dare turn his head to look down at her, but an instant later he heard once more the heavy double report of the short-barreled scatter-gun.

A huge granite slab loomed ahead. Quist maneuvered the reins, swung his leaders to the right. The coach skidded, swayed like some drunken thing. Tire irons screeched on buried chunks of rock. There came a crashing of branches as the coach crushed a small mesquite tree. Sparks flew from the slipping hoofs of the horses.

The stage dipped suddenly from the shoulder. Quist was nearly thrown from his seat. He braced himself, swung the horses to the left again, straightened them out.

Again they were back on the road, running free. A curve

showed ahead. The coach made it. Now the way climbed. Quist employed his whip. The horses didn't slacken speed an instant. The coach bounced and swerved up the incline toward two precipitous granite bluffs, which showed a wide passage as they were approached. Horses and coach entered Bisnaga Pass, the rock walls flashing past on either side. The pass ran almost straight and beyond, hazy in the distance, Quist could see open country and blue sky once more. He started to slow the coach.

The vehicle halted, the horses steaming and panting, rolling their eyes. Quist glanced at the girl. She'd lost her hat and the hair was tumbled about her face. She started putting it in place. She looked a trifle pale and shaken. Quist said, "You all right?"

She nodded. "I'm—I'm just wondering why my father—ever —ever bothered with grading roads." Her voice sounded tremulous, breathless. "With—with drivers like you to be had—men who don't care about level going, we could have run the route straight over the Arcanums."

Quist laughed shortly. "You did your part. That shotgun work—"

"But what were we shooting at? I just aimed in the general direction of your shots. I couldn't see anybody, but that roadblock—"

"Which wasn't a landslide as you thought. I didn't see anybody either, but the roadblock didn't look good to me. I figured if there was anybody up there, I'd shoot first, take 'em by surprise and keep them ducked down, until we got around that barrier—"

"I heard somebody shooting up there, of course, but why—"

"That man-made landslide was supposed to halt the coach while the rocks were rolled away from the road. I had to think fast. We couldn't go over the rocks, but there was a chance we could circumvent them. Your horses are good climbers."

"I'm still asking, why should anyone want to stop the stage?"

"Ever hear of bandits—road-agents—Miss Callister?"

50

"Of course"—impatiently—"but we carried nothing worth stealing. There's just mail in the strongbox—" She paused. "What are you doing?"

Quist had got his satchel, opened it and secured the mate to his underarm gun, which he slipped into a coat pocket with a handful of forty-four cartridges. He ejected empty shells and reloaded the holster weapon. "You stay here, out of sight behind the coach. Keep that shotgun handy. Better reload it. I'm heading back to that roadblock and see what I can learn—"

"I'll go with you—"

"You'll stay here," Quist curtly interrupted. "If I don't return in a reasonable length of time, you drive on and inform the sheriff what's happened."

The girl bridled. "Now look here, Mister Gregory, I'm not accustomed to taking orders from men who work for me—"

"For the present," Quist interrupted, "you'd best get used to being ordered around. I do things my way. And I've a hunch you won't be hiring me. Now stay here with that shotgun like I said."

He didn't give the girl time to reply but started back up the pass on foot. Ten minutes later the way opened up. By this time he was perspiring freely. "Damn," he grumbled, "I never did care for walking in the open country."

He pushed steadily on, rounding curves in the roadway, ears and eyes alert for the first sign of the enemy. Glancing once toward the sky, he saw the sun was swinging well to the west. He pounded on, right hand never far from the gun in his underarm holster, his booted feet raising small clouds of dust at every step.

He followed the road around an upthrust jagged chunk of dark gray granite and saw the roadblock ahead. It looked as before—just a big heap of tumbled rock and brush. He peered cautiously around the big rock and up the slope. There wasn't any movement to be seen.

Abruptly, Quist drew his six-shooter and broke into a zigzag-ging run toward the slope, half expecting shots to come crashing about his ears. But nothing of the sort took place. If there was anybody up there, they were keeping well hidden. After a time he relaxed, and moved less cautiously up the slope, wending his way around boulders and past stunted mesquite and low-grow-ing prickly pear. "I reckon they fanned tails out of here," Quist mused.

Twenty minutes of examining the slope produced nothing, and he was about to start down when he spied horse droppings just beyond a big irregularly shaped block of granite. He examined the earth with narrowing eyes, moving about in a stooping posi-tion. After a minute of searching for sign, he climbed with some difficulty to the top of the rock where he could peer over the sur-rounding country.

Seventy-five yards below, on the road, he could see the heap of rocks that had been intended to halt the stage long enough to —to do exactly what? He frowned. His gaze followed the road toward the north. At times it was partially blotted from view where it curved about jagged rock. Then, still farther to the north he saw two riders, pushing their horses furiously along the trail. They were too far off to be recognized, even if he'd been familiar with the inhabitants of this country. The riders were leading be-hind them a third horse.

Quist studied the two fleeing figures a moment. One of them appeared to be somewhat slumped in the saddle, as though he'd been injured. "I wonder if one of us did hit a man with our wild shooting." He pondered. "Sort of looks that way. But why the third horse? Were there three men, or was the other animal in-tended to carry somebody off? . . ."

A deep frown creased his forehead. He watched the rapidly riding figures a moment longer, then slid down from the rock. He stood there a moment, rolling a cigarette and lighting it. Tobacco smoke drifted on the breeze and a certain chill had entered the air. The lowering sun was putting the mountain side in shadow.

"Guess I'd best get back to the coach," Quist said, and rounded the big rock on the opposite side. Then he stopped short, a slow breath exhaling from his lips, and his eyes narrowed. He said, after an instant, "I guess we hit more than one hombre."

Almost directly at his feet lay the crumpled body of a man. The earth beneath was sodden with dark blood. The fellow lay on his face, one outstretched arm resting awkwardly against the trunk of a small mesquite, the other doubled beneath the body. The dead man's six-shooter lay a foot away as though it had fallen from his grasp as he went down.

Stooping, Quist gently turned over the body, recognizing at once the lifeless features. The dead man was Yoakum who had taken the stage from Black Ore Springs to Woods Diggings. Quist went through the man's pockets. They produced little of interest—pocketknife, nearly depleted plug of tobacco, a filthy bandanna, two slot machine checks, two silver dollars and thirty-five cents in change. No letters or papers of any sort. The bullet that killed him had emerged from the front of his body. It wasn't a pleasant sight.

Quist moved the body to its original position and studied the wound in the back, reconstructing the scene mentally: "Yoakum was crouched down here, shielded by rock and brush. One of my shots struck this granite rock at his back, flattened and then ricochetted, tearing into his body. And finishing him pronto. Lord, what a hole! I'll bet he never knew what struck him." Quist's frown deepened. "Pure luck, that shot. But why did those hombres want to hold up the stage? What's back of this business?"

He was still pondering the question as he retraced his steps back to the road and started in the direction of Bisnaga Pass. He was halfway to the coach when he met Alexandra Callister approaching, the shotgun cradled under one arm. She began, somewhat defiantly, "You were so long, I thought I'd better see what was happening. And let's get it clear, Gregory, I don't want any more of this giving orders from you." Her chin lifted, eyes hot.

Quist smiled thinly. "I was talking for your own good. Didn't know what I might run into. All right, you've made your point. You're stubborn and you're hot-tempered. You're going to have your own way in spite of hell and high water. That's settled. We'll forget it."

Her face crimsoned. Then she checked the impulsive words surging to her lips. "I'm glad to hear it's settled," she answered stiffly. "And now, if it's not asking too much, will you tell me if you learned anything back there?"

"I see you found your hat," he evaded. "Saw it on my way out. Intended to pick it up on the way back—"

"Did you learn anything?" she insisted.

"Yes," he replied tersely. "I learned, when hiding out, a man should never have his back to a rock, like Yoakum—"

"Yoakum? What about him?"

"I'm asking you. What do you know about him? Ever have any trouble with him?"

She shook her head. "I don't think I've ever even spoken to the man. I just know he has a reputation of being a no-good bum and never holds a job long. What about him?"

"He's still up on that slope," Quist said. "Probably got a horse right after he left the stage and raced to meet two other men who had constructed that road barrier. He likely gave them information as to how many were riding the stage and so on—what to expect. There was sign of three horses there. Also blood on the earth where one of the men mounted—"

"You mean one of our shots hit somebody?" The girl stared at him, wide-eyed.

"Two somebodys," Quist said shortly. "As I said, Yoakum is

54

still up on that slope. He won't be leaving unless somebody carries him away."

"You—you're saying I might have killed him?"

Quist shook his head. "A buckshot wouldn't have a wound like Yoakum got. It was one of my forty-fours. You may have pinged one of Yoakum's pards." He gave her further details, concluding, "Those riders were too far off for me to tell much about 'em, or what they were wearing. Denims, sombreros. That's about all I could make out. And riding hard. When we hit town we'll have to inform the sheriff."

"I'll see that word's sent to the sheriff at Black Ore Springs. Where it took place is in Acacia County. Arcanum City is in Pitahaya County." She shook her head. "But he left the stage at Wood's Diggings. He must have made awfully good time—"

"Likely there was a horse waiting for him. And a horse can go where a stage can't, take shortcuts."

"I guess you're right." The girl frowned. "But I still can't see any reason for holding up the stage. Bandits generally inform themselves ahead of time when a stage is carrying anything valuable. And we've had no trouble with stage robbers for years now."

They walked toward the stage. "Want me to continue driving?" Quist asked.

The girl shook her head as she climbed to the driver's seat, while Quist mounted at the opposite side. "You just keep that shotgun handy in case of more trouble." Her lips curved slightly. "My objection to your driving, you don't like to keep on the ground long enough at a time. I'll swear there were moments when all four wheels were free of the earth."

"So you probably won't hire me regular then," Quist smiled.

"I've got to think about it," the girl said seriously.

"Don't forget you still owe me twenty dollars."

The girl snapped at him, "I don't see how you can make jokes when a man has just been killed."

55

"Maybe," Quist said shortly, "I make jokes to forget I was responsible for his death. Lord knows I hate killing—and killers. Certainly I'm not feeling good about that business right now. But you'd best realize, Miss Callister, if I hadn't acted as I did, maybe it would be you or I that was dead now."

"I know. I'm sorry, Gregory." She forced a rather wan smile. "All right, I owe you twenty dollars."

"And don't, please, forget my rebate on the fare."

The girl got the horses going again. Ten minutes later they had emerged from Bisnaga Pass and started a gradual descent along a rocky grade that offered several hairpin turns.

The sun was behind the mountains by the time they reached Honey-Pod Ranch station. Honey-pod mesquite trees grew thickly through this section. Fresh horses and two attendants waited before the whitewashed station. The girl drew the horses to a halt.

The two station men glanced up at Quist then started to unharness. "You're late, Miss Alex," one of the men commented. "Me'n Jed was beginnin' to think something had gone wrong."

"It did," the girl explained briefly. "I had to hire another guard, Tom. This is Gregory, boys." She gave their names. Quist and the men exchanged nods. The girl continued and told what had happened, while the men stared in amazement and looked with new respect at Quist. ". . . and, Tom," the girl finished, "you or Jed will have to ride to Black Ore Springs and let the sheriff know what happened. I'll see that you get overtime . . ."

"It might be a good idea, while you're there," Quist put in, "to ask some questions. See if you can learn who Yoakum has been parding with lately, and if anybody with a gunshot wound has showed up. I've got a hunch your guard, Charley, who quit, might be mixed into the business some way."

"That's a right idea," Tom replied. "I'll talk to old Buzzard Greer. Usually he knows what goes on around a town. . . ."

The fresh horses were ready. Alexandra Callister picked up the lines. There were shouts of good-bye and the coach rolled away from the station, gathering speed as it moved across the again flat terrain.

Quist commented, "I didn't see any signs of a ranch at Honey-Pod, or is it farther back?"

"It was my father's first spread. He used to raise horses there. Now it's part of the Box-VC. The old buildings still stand, farther west. But there's just the stage station in use now."

It became darker. Twilight lingered only a few minutes, then the coach was rolling on through the night. Stars blinked into being overhead. It was too early for the moon to show. Quist was glad not to be driving now, but the girl appeared familiar with every inch of the road, swinging around curves at the right moment and skillfully avoiding bad spots on the route.

A brief halt was made at Bisnaga Creek, where the stage station stood beside a narrow stream of water crossed by a plank bridge. Fresh horses were harnessed in and the coach rolled on through the night. It was around eight-thirty when the lights of Arcanum City shone against the dark sky, spreading a faint glow which silhouetted the tops of buildings.

The girl asked Quist if he planned to stay at the hotel for the night. Quist said that he did. When they reached the town, she tooled the team along a throughfare, which she told him was Mesquite Street, until they came to the main street. The stage station stood at the corner of Main (once known as Pitahaya) and Mesquite. Here the girl drove the coach directly to a corral and barn at the rear of the station, saying to Quist, "The hotel is just across Main."

Attendants emerged from the stables to unharness the weary animals and water them. While the girl was answering questions relative to her tardy arrival, Quist secured his grip and dropped down from the coach on the opposite side, then started off.

For a moment the girl didn't miss him. She turned suddenly, then, calling, "Will I see you tomorrow, Gregory?"

Quist spoke over his shoulder, without breaking stride, "You can't avoid it; I'm aiming to collect that twenty, y'know."

He didn't wait for the girl's reply, but strode on.

VI

MOST of the shops and stores were closed along Main Street, but quite a number of lights still shone from buildings. Quist paused a moment on the corner of Main and Mesquite, whipping with his sombrero the dust of travel from his clothing. The street was unpaved and rutted, but there were plank sidewalks on either side. Pedestrians strode along the street. There were horses and wagons standing at an almost unbroken line of hitchracks.

On the opposite corner stood the hotel, a big rectangular two-story building constructed of rock and adobe, its front wall rising flush from the inner edge of the sidewalk. There wasn't any porch, but running along the front second story, with a door opening on to it, was a long wooden gallery, with roof overhead. A sign nailed to the gallery railing proclaimed it to be the Arcanum House. Below the gallery, four entrances gave access to the hotel, the one nearest the corner having a sign over it, reading Arcanum Bar. The other doors Quist judged opened on the lobby, a parlor and a ladies' sitting room.

Quist settled his hat back on his head, picked up his satchel and crossed over. A couple of men glanced up curiously from chairs when he entered the lobby and approached the desk. The clerk, a fussy-looking individual wearing a celluloid wing collar and sideburns showing touches of black hair dye, spun his register as Quist stepped up.

58

"A room, sir?" he asked deferentially.

"That's the general idea," Quist nodded. "One with a cross breeze if possible."

The clerk beamed toothily. "You'll get it, sir. What we consider our very best room. Number 19. You're fortunate—or shall I say we're fortunate in having you—it was just vacated this afternoon. A corner room. Just what you'll want, I hope. I'm so pleased. I always say there's nothing like pleasing a patron—"

"A key goes with it, I suppose," Quist said dryly, scribbling his name on the register page.

"Why, naturally, Mr.—er—" He reversed the register to read Quist's writing. His jaw dropped slightly. He looked up, staring at Quist. "Mis-ter Quist! We'd heard you were coming here, but—"

"Where'd you hear it?"

The clerk's pallid face flushed, he gnawed nervously on one fingernail. "We-ell, now, Mr. Quist, I just can't say offhand. It was just sort of rumored around, let us say."

"All right"—genially—"lets. But who rumored it?"

"I really couldn't tell you. One hears these things—" He broke off. "I still don't understand. There's been no train for over two hours, and the next one not due until—"

"I walked," Quist cut in, "or just let us say I ran all the way."

The clerk looked uncertain. "Well"—weakly—"if you say so, Mr. Quist."

"And the key?" Quist hinted.

The clerk twisted around, removed a key from a slot and placed it on the desk. "I can't begin to say how pleased we are to have you with us—"

"Don't bother trying then. And now if you'll have the bar send up a dozen bottles of beer, I'll be much obliged. And I *don't* want *cold* beer."

"I'll take care of it, Mr. Quist." He craned his neck out over the

59

desk as Quist started to ascend the stairs lifting from the lobby.

As he moved up the steps, Quist heard him tell the men in the lobby, "I'll never believe in a hundred years that he *walked* here. You know what? I'll bet a pretty that he came on the stage-coach. . . ."

An oil lamp was suspended from the ceiling on the second floor lighting the small hallway, and Quist had no trouble locating room number 19 at one front corner. A couple of feet from it was a closed door leading to the second-story gallery. Quist inserted his key in the room lock and opened the door, entered and closed it again. Some faint light entered the windows from the street and Quist saw on a dresser an oil lamp with a white globe. He scratched a match, touched it to the wick. With chimney and globe replaced, he turned to survey the room.

It was a larger room than was generally found in cattle-town hotels. There were even draperies of some sort and shades at the front windows. A smaller window was located in one side wall. There was a mirror over a commode, on which stood a water pitcher and basin. The floor was covered with a carpet of some complex design. There were two straight-backed chairs, a rocker and a double bed. A clothes stand stood between commode and dresser.

"A plumb elegant room," Quist commented in some surprise, as he crossed and drew down the shades. He came back to his satchel on the bed, opened it and produced shaving tackle; his coat and holstered six-shooter were hung on the foot of the bed. Then he removed his sombrero and shirt. A knock came at the door which opened at Quist's bidding. A man from the bar came in bearing a tray of bottled beer. Quist directed him to place it on the commode and tipped him. The man withdrew, but Quist hadn't missed the curiosity in the fellow's eyes.

Quist applied the opener to the cup-shaped stopper on a bottle and, disregarding the two glasses on the tray, tilted the bottle to his lips. When he had finished the bottle and opened a second, he began to shave.

He had donned a clean shirt and found a fresh bandanna, when there came another knock on the door. Quist moved toward his holstered gun at the end of the bed and called, "Come on. It isn't locked."

The door opened, closed again. A man stood there, wearing on his open vest the badge of a deputy sheriff. He was a very small man and rawboned. And wiry. He looked as tough and durable as a length of well-seasoned rawhide. He had brick-red hair, a sinewy jaw and steady blue eyes. He wasn't more than thirty and his boots carried a mirror-like polish.

"Mr. Quist?" Quist nodded. "I'm Rod Larrabee."

"Not *Red* Larrabee?" Quist smiled.

"Should be, shoudn't it?" the small man grinned. "But it's plain Rod, in spite of my hair. Could I talk to you for a few minutes?"

"I don't know why not. Grab a chair. Have a beer?"

Larrabee repeated Quist's words, "I don't know why not."

Quist shook hands with him and opened a couple of bottles of beer. Larrabee refused a glass and dropped into a chair, tilting his sombrero to the back of his head. He said, "I've heard a lot about your work, from time to time. I was glad to hear you were headed here, so I'd get a chance to meet you—"

"Where'd you hear it?" Quist dropped on the bed.

The red head scowled thoughtfully. "Reckon I can't say for sure, Mr. Quist. I think the news just got circulated around. I believe a man from your railroad—Mr. Fletcher?—first mentioned you might come here, and then the idea sort of builded. Folks have been watching the trains—"

"Any folks in particular?"

Larrabee carefully placed his bottle on the floor near his chair, and wiped his lips with a bandanna. He seemed to be a very neat

61

man. "Folks who are interested," he said finally, "and that covers a good many in Arcanum City. They're taking sides, one way or another, figuring with your rep maybe you can settle things."

"What things?"

Larrabee looked surprised. "Why, I figured you had the story. Well, you know, the business of who died first, Anne or Vance Callister? Vance's daughter, Alexandra, has a lot of friends who want things to go her way. 'Course, that applies to the other side too."

"So I understand. But that's not what you came here to tell me. What's on your mind, Deputy? How'd you locate me so fast?"

Larrabee laughed shortly. "Maybe that was sort of by accident. You see, I was talking to Alex—Miss Callister—and she said there'd been some trouble on the drive down and that she'd hired a man named Gregory—"

"That's my first name." Quist chuckled.

"I realize that now. Anyway, she said that this Gregory had gone to the hotel, and I figured to come and get the details of exactly what happened direct from you. Alex said you seemed reliable, but inclined to be bossy." He grinned his infectious grin. "She didn't like that and she's going to be riled when she learns you slipped one over on her. It all sounded sort of mysterious to me, so I aimed to see what was up. When I hit the hotel I looked at Nelly's register—"

"Who?" Quist frowned.

"Nelly Grimes—the clerk down in the lobby. His initials are N. L., but folks got to calling him Nelly." He added dryly, "I ain't the least idea why, have you?"

"Well," Quist conceded, "he is a trifle old-maidish."

Larrabee nodded. "When I saw the register I realized right off what had happened. So here I am. Exactly what did occur on that drive?"

Quist told the story. A scowl came to Larrabee's face. "What do you think was back of that attempt to stop the stage?"

Quist threw out one word that was more of a question, "Bandits?"

The small man said impatiently, "Bosh!"

"You tell me then."

"Right. Look here, there are two factions claiming Vance Callister's estate; on one side, Alex Callister; on the other, Helen and Everett Bancroft. It's to be settled at the fall court, if you don't turn up something first—"

"Which I'm not at all sure I'll be able to do. But go on."

"Suppose one of the claimants disappeared suddenly. That would leave clear going for the other side. Alex has no other relatives—all dead—so the Bancrofts would have clear sailing."

Quist studied the small deputy. "In short, you're saying that the stage was to be stopped for the purpose of kidnaping Miss Callister. Do you actually believe that?"

Larrabee flushed a little. "Yes, sir, I guess I do."

"So you're saying the Bancrofts planned the business?"

Now Larrabee hesitated. "Dammit," he said uneasily, "I hate to make an accusation like that. Helen Bancroft seems to be on the square."

"But her brother isn't?"

"I'd hate to say that too"—awkwardly. "I don't know a thing against him. He appears all right. Never really talked to him much. He's only been here a mite over a month. And just because people are claiming an estate, doesn't mean they're ready to commit violence to win. I got to admit that. Maybe that attempt had nothing to do with Alex."

"What was back of it then?" Quist took a swallow of beer.

"Maybe somebody was aiming to stop *you* from coming here."

"I thought of that. That's why I didn't arrive directly by train but took a roundabout route, with stage part way. But who

63

would be trying to stop me—Miss Callister or the Bancrofts?"

Larrabee looked shocked. "Not Alex. Cripes, if she'd had anything like that in mind, she was holding the shotgun while you were driving—" He broke off. "Not that Alex would ever dream of—"

"No?" Quist snapped. "Maybe it was planned to shoot me in the back while I was rolling rocks from the road—"

"No, look here, Quist—"

"But of course, she didn't know my name was Quist then. Could be she thought I'd missed the stage."

The small man's face flamed and he started to rise from his chair. "You're all wrong, Quist, if you're suspecting Alex—"

"Keep your breeches on," Quist said curtly. "It's plain you're on Alex Callister's side. You'd like to see her get the money. Why, I don't know. Maybe you're planning to marry her if she does—"

"Damn you, Quist." Larrabee bounced from his chair and started for the door, his face flaming.

Quist moved lithely from the bed, seized Larrabee's arm, flung him around. For a moment, the small man resisted him and Quist was astonished at the strength in the man's wiry frame, before he allowed himself to be flung, panting, back in his chair, reluctant admiration for Quist's muscles showing in his eyes.

"I didn't invite you up here," Quist said savagely. "You came up of your own accord. Now, by God, you'll stay here until I finish talking. I'm asking you, did you ever plan to marry Alex Callister?"

"That's none of your damned business," Larrabee growled.

"All right, you answered me," Quist said curtly.

"But, dammit, I never did—"

"Never wanted to?"

Larrabee opened his mouth, closed it again. Then, with an effort the small man kept his voice steady, "What I wanted or

64

didn't want has nothing to do with it—"

"You think not?" Quist sneered. "Let's put it this way. Maybe you've never said anything to her. Maybe she never considered you, even. But she might consider you if I could be put out of the way and you—"

"You're going too far, Quist." Larrabee's voice trembled.

"You're smart," Quist pushed relentlessly on, as though he'd not heard the interruption. "It would occur to you that I might arrive by coach. You could have had friends watching both trains and coach. A rider could have been sent ahead when I got off the train at Wolverton. A relay of horses. It's not impossible, is it, Larrabee, with big money at stake?"

Fists clenched, face white with anger, Larrabee rose from his chair. "I'm leaving, Quist—" his voice trembled—"and I'm warning you not to stop me again. As deputy-sheriff here—"

Quist said in a normal tone of voice, "I suppose the dining room downstairs is closed by this time. My stomach feels as though my throat had been cut."

The small man swung back from the door, frowning, staring.

Quist smiled apologetically. "I'm sorry, Rod. I can be an awful bastard at times, but it's my way of finding out things. I don't seem to learn any other way. But I've got to learn who I can trust and who I can't. I feel pretty sure about you, now. I could tell from the way you acted, you're on the level. Maybe we can work together."

Larrabee came back into the room, jaw dropping, disbelief in his blue eyes. "You—you mean, that was just an act?"

"Something like that. Let's forget it. And I haven't had any supper yet."

A slow smile crossed the small man's face. "I guess Alex isn't the only one that got taken in today. Look, there's an all-night restaurant a couple of doors from here. They fry a pretty good steak. I'll take you there—"

"Good. Just a minute while I get this shirt buttoned. Oh, yes, and you'd best persuade Miss Callister not to drive any more trips on that stage route."

Larrabee looked up sharply. "You agree with me then it might have been a plot to kidnap her?"

"Thought so, right along. Tried to persuade her it was just road-agents, but I guess I wasn't too successful."

"Then you think the Bancrofts—?"

"I think nothing of the kind," Quist said crisply. "I know nothing about either Bancroft, except hearsay and—" He broke off and reached for the holstered gun on the end of the bed, started to strap on the harness.

"That's quite an outfit," Larrabee commented.

"It's the best I've been able to work out, anyway," Quist replied.

"Your own invention?"

"I had it made up for me. It's mighty convenient. With this holster you just jerk your gun straight out, through this open side, instead of up and out as you would with a holster at your side. That might save a fraction of a second in drawing—and sometimes that fraction is the difference between life and death." With the harness adjusted he made a couple of draws to demonstrate. "See?"

"But what holds the gun in that holster?"

"A flat steel spring, sewed inside the leather, holds the gun in place until it's drawn." Quist slipped into his coat then procured some cartridges from his satchel which he slipped into his pocket.

"Don't you wear a ca'tridge belt?"

Quist shook his head. "Too heavy. Any man that can't do his job with what's in his cylinder and a few extra, hasn't any business carrying a gun."

"Hardly shows under your coat, does it?"

"I get my coats tailor-made and the tailor makes allowances.

66

They're generally lightweight material, in case the weather is hot when I'm wearing 'em. Come on, let's go get that chow."

VII

ROD LARRABEE made a lunch of coffee and cigarettes while Quist worked his way through a steak and fried potatoes. "I'm being frank with you," Quist said through bites, "when I tell you, Rod, that I've not the least idea what I can do here. But I'm here on orders from my company. All I can do is pick up details, learn what's to be learned, and after talking to people, wait for a break. But I still think it's a job for the medics to unravel. Incidentally, I understand that the doctor who claims Callister's wife died first, was fired on. What's the story?"

Larrabee said, "Maybe I'd better go back a little and see what you know." Quist nodded assent and Rod went on, "The Box-VC cook discovered the bodies, headed for town and got Sheriff Kiernan, my boss. Jake Kiernan is the name. Jake couldn't get Doctor Forbes, Callister's regular doctor—"

"Why should Callister have a regular doctor? Was he sick—?"

"Not real serious. Some sort of belly-ache or indigestion. Anyway, Doc Forbes was out assisting on a new baby. It was a difficult delivery—Mrs. Uzzell at the Rafter-U—and Forbes didn't get back until late the following night—actually it was three in the morning. Anyway, when Jake couldn't get Forbes, he grabbed old Doc Luke Iverson, poured him into a saddle—"

"I understand this Iverson is something of a drunk."

Larrabee's face clouded. "And it's too damn bad, too. Used to be a right smart doctor. Then his wife died a few years back and he kind of went to pieces. Practice went to hell and so on. Eventually Forbes came to town and took over. Only those who can't

67

pay their bills or don't intend to, call Iverson nowdays. Anyway, they got Iverson out to the Box-VC, but there was nothing much Iverson could do, with Anne and Vance Callister both dead, and the gun still in her hand."

Quist nodded. "I understand it appeared to be a cut-and-dried proposition. Murder and then suicide."

"*Appeared* is right. The following day the inquest was held. In Doc Forbes' absence, Luke Iverson took over. He'd held the job of coroner previously so it was an old story to him. The verdict came in, murder and suicide. There was no one to be apprehended, so the burial took place the following day. And that's all anyone thought about it. It wasn't until the will was read that Doc Iverson scrambled things by stating, in his opinion, that Anne Callister had been first to die. Folks thought that was just the woozy idea of an old drunk, but he stuck to his guns. So that's what has brought about the tangled situation. He'd examined the bodies and should know, but could he be depended on? After all, folks said, it was Anne Callister who was found with the gun in her hand. Certainly she had killed Callister before killing herself. So there you are, Mr. Quist."

"Let's forget the 'mister,' and just where am I? All right. A couple of days ago somebody took a shot at this Doc Iverson. Why?"

The small man scowled. "I'm damned if I can say. Iverson lives in a shack across the tracks. He had to give up his old house in town. Lives out there among a few scattered Mexican adobes, surrounded by mesquite and cactus. Maybe he likes drinking alone, I don't know. I will say, the Mexicans swear by him—"

"So *they* didn't shoot at him," Quist hinted.

"And I can't say who did. All Iverson knows is that a forty-four slug came through his window, though it didn't come anywhere near him. Then he *thinks* he heard somebody getting away fast. He was groggy at the time. It didn't bother him any.

68

Maybe he doesn't care if anybody plugs him. It was one of the Mexicans who brought the news to the sheriff the next morning. I went out to see him then."

"Did your sheriff investigate?"

"Jake left it to me."

"How'd you know it was a forty-four?"

"The slug hit a mirror and imbedded itself in the wall behind. I dug it out."

"I like a forty-four myself," Quist commented.

"Quite a few of them used hereabouts," Larrabee said. "After all, it makes sense. Why not use a ca'tridge that can be used in both six-shooters and rifles?"

Quist nodded. "Exactly." He took a sip of black coffee, his eyes narrowing. "Let's suppose for a minute that forty-four slug had killed Doctor Iverson. What would happen?"

"He'd be dead, that's all." The small man squinted curiously at Quist. "What could happen?"

"For one thing," Quist pointed out, "he'd not be alive to testify that Anne Callister died first."

"You're saying—" and Larrabee's face colored a little—"that somebody was trying to throw the dice in the Bancrofts' favor. Now wait, I'm not jumping to conclusions this time. Damn! I should have thought of that. I'm getting slow-witted I guess."

"A man can't think of everything. Who else besides the Bancrofts want to see them get the money?"

"I wouldn't want to go on record as naming anybody, Greg, with any feeling of sureness. Not anybody that would try murder, at least."

"All right, we'll forget it for the time being." Quist called for another cup of coffee and the proprietor of the restaurant brought it. He and Larrabee were the only ones in the restaurant now. They sat at a corner table and the proprietor was out in his kitchen most of the time. Quist twisted a brown-paper cigarette.

"What sort of man was Vance Callister? Any enemies?"

"I imagine so. A man doesn't make as much money as he made without creating grudges along the way. He was a big man, what I'd call hard. Square, of course, but hard just the same. And arrogant at times, inclined to ride roughshod over anybody who opposed his ideas. He was like a lot of big men who've made money."

"Ever hear anybody threaten his life or anything of the sort?"

"Can't say I have. I've known men to be mad at him of course."

"Can you name any?"

Larrabee's eyes evaded Quist's. "No, I couldn't say offhand."

"His wife, Anne?"

The deputy laughed, sounding rather relieved. He shook his head. "You figuring somebody prompted her to doing it, and then in a fit of remorse she killed herself?"

"I didn't say that," Quist replied mildly. "It was your idea." He added, "Anyway, you wouldn't want it that way, would you?"

"What do you mean?"

"Face it, Rod," Quist said quietly, "you want it cut-and-dried that Anne died first, without any doubts. You're on Alex Callister's side all the way."

Larrabee nodded soberly. "You never said a truer word, Greg. Just the same I wouldn't—"

"I know you wouldn't," Quist cut in. "I wouldn't be talking this way if I didn't. I'm just trying to make you use your head and look at all angles. Don't even trust your own thoughts until you've checked 'em twice. Just how did Callister happen to marry Anne, anyway? Do you know anything about that?"

The small man shook his head. "It came as a surprise to a lot of people, after the way things had been going—"

"What things?"

Marshaling his thoughts, Larrabee didn't answer at once, then, "Helen Bancroft came here two years ago and bought the hotel—"

"Did she have cash money?"

"That I couldn't say. The sale was put through to settle the estate of the former owner. I think the bank handled the deal. Maybe they could tell you She was quite popular from the first."

"What sort of a woman is she?"

"A looker, to hear folks tell it. I guess she is all right. Not as pretty as Alex though—"

"You wouldn't be biased, would you?" Quist asked, smiling.

"Admitted. Miss Bancroft's an older woman than Alex—probably close to thirty. Maybe older. But she's considerable woman to look at and friendly with everybody. She certainly cleaned up that old Arcanum House in a hurry. Anyway, I guess Vance Callister was right smitten with her, and while nothing was actually said, it was rumored around he was set to marry her. Then about a year back, her sister Anne came here to help her run the hotel. Gradually Callister changed his allegiance, and about two months back he married Anne, to everybody's surprise. It all seemed to happen sort of sudden. Leastwise, it seemed that way."

"What sort of woman was Anne—like her sister?"

Larrabee shook his head. "Helen is blonde and laughs a lot. The friendly type that a lot of men like. Anne was a smaller woman, sort of round and—well you might call her defenceless-looking. Kind of shy and demure and quiet, very ladylike. Brown eyes and darker hair."

'And yet she killed her husband. I always said the shrinking-violet type is the most dangerous."

"It would look that way."

"Where does Everett Bancroft come into the picture?"

"He arrived later, after Anne had married Callister. Helen needed a day clerk and he got the job. Nelly Grimes just works nights. I suppose Everett helps in other ways too."

"Maybe he's part owner, in the hotel business."

"I never heard that he was. He's more like Helen than Anne.

71

Not a bad looking cuss, friendly and so on."

Quist shot his next question: "How did Alex get along with her father?"

The small man frowned. "Well, to tell the truth—" He paused. "I think that's something you'd better ask Alex, Greg."

Quist nodded. "I'll do that." He put down his napkin. "Let's drift out and look over the town. I think I can stand a drink too." He crossed to the counter running along one wall, left some money on it and Larrabee followed him out to the street.

The town appeared quiet. There were only a few pedestrians along the walks and still fewer horses and vehicles at hitchracks. Quist and the deputy strolled up one side of Main and back the other, stopping at two different saloons to get drinks. A few men were introduced to Quist at various points. There were several cross streets bisecting Main: Concho, Mesquite, Coyotero, Pima; a block north of Main, running parallel to it, was Cottonwood Street, largely given over to residences. The First National Bank of Arcanum City, built of brick, stood on the north corner of Main and Mesquite, just across from the hotel. A secondary hotel called the Miners' & Cattlemen's was at the corner of Concho and Main. There were a couple of general stores, a gunsmith shop and various other places of commercial enterprise.

"Quite a town you got here," Quist commented.

"It's growing fast, too"—local pride in Larrabee's tones.

"Much mining hereabouts?"

Larrabee shook his head. "Not any more—not south of the Arcanum Mountains. There used to be considerable. But most of the ore comes from over near Wood's Diggings and Black Ore Springs. Mostly cattle around here now."

"Which reminds me," Quist said, "I suppose I'll have to have some business with the sheriff up there, on account of Yoakum's death. There'll be an inquest and all that."

"I don't figure you'll have any trouble. Sheriff Burks of Acacia

72

County is a pretty good head. I'll send him word that you're here and can be seen at any time he needs you. We're good friends and he'll take my word for things. Besides I want him to dig into that business and see what he can learn about Yoakum or anyone else that might have had a hand in that business."

"What about that guard, Charley somebody-or-other?"

"I plan to have Burks dig into his activities too. Charley Biggs, his name is. He used to live here. Then after Alex hired him, he left Arcanum City. He never amounted to much around here, and Alex only hired him when she couldn't get anybody else. But don't bother, I'll tend to things."

Quist smiled. "You talk like you were the sheriff instead of his deputy."

"Could be," the small man returned. "Jake Kiernan leaves things pretty much to me to handle."

"What's the matter with Kiernan? His politics running to fat?"

A slight frown crossed Larrabee's face. "I wouldn't say that," he replied loyally. "Jake's been a good man for Pitahaya County. There's no crime to speak of, aside from—well, to tell the truth, Jake's no spring chicken. He's worked hard in his day. He won't run for office again, and he'd like to see me voted in next election. So he lets me handle a lot of responsibilities."

They walked in silence for a few minutes. Quist said suddenly, "What became of the gun Anne Callister used on her husband and herself?"

"It's at the office. We're keeping it until the case is brought to court. You want to see it?" Quist said he did. Larrabee said, "We'll have to turn back to Pima Street. Maybe Jake will be at the office. You can meet him too."

They turned and crossed Main, their boot-heels clumping hollowly on the plank sidewalks, as they headed east, past Perkins & Meek's General Store, now dark, past the Blue Star Restaurant and the Gold Dollar Saloon. The sheriff's office was a long

73

rectangular building built of adobe, at the corner of Main and Pima, its length running along Pima, with a corral at the rear, facing the T.N. & A.S. tracks. A wooden awning extended above the entrance to uprights rising from the outer edge of the side-walk, and nailed to the edge of the awning was a wooden sign: Sheriff's Office, Pitahaya County.

Larrabee led the way across a small porch raised a few inches from the sidewalk, opened the door of the office and stepped within. An oil lamp turned low burned on the top of a roll-top desk near the window. The floor was of well-scrubbed pine boards. There was a cuspidor near the desk, three straight-backed chairs, and a cot at one wall with carefully folded blankets. A door at the rear, at present closed, led to the cell block. A cast-iron stove with chimney running through the ceiling, stood in one corner. The walls held a coatrack, a gunrack, a topographical map of the county and a couple of calendars from packing houses. A small iron safe stood at the foot of the cot.

"You sleep here?" Quist asked.

"Yeah. Jake stays at a boardinghouse. Probably there now, or at the Arcanum Bar."

"Not married, eh?"

"He's an old bach—though it looked for a spell—" The small man broke off. "I'll get Callister's gun for you in a jiffy."

He crossed to the safe, knelt down and twirled the combination knob. The heavy door swung back under his hand, and reaching in he produced a six-shooter which he handed up to Quist. Then he got to his feet.

It was of forty-four caliber with a walnut butt. Quist noted the initials VC stamped in the wood. "This was Callister's own gun, eh, Rod?"

The small man nodded. "The supposition is that Callister and his wife had an argument. She yanked the gun from his holster and plugged him, before he realized what she was doing, then

74

shot herself. The gun was still gripped in her hand when the bodies were found."

"Were you there at the time?"

Larrabee shook his head. "Jake figured he'd best go himself, that night. It was him got the doctor. I stayed in town in case anything came up."

"And I suppose the sheriff took charge of the gun."

"The only time it's been out of this office was at the inquest. It's been in the safe ever since."

Quist was examining the gun, twirling the cylinder. "Three loaded ca'tridges," he said half to himself, "and three empty shells. I suppose Callister just loaded with five and left his hammer resting on an empty."

"I don't think there's any doubt about it. That's the way everybody I know handles his six-shooter."

"Did he do much shooting? I mean, was Callister the type that's always yanking his gun to show off how he can hit a bottle or a sign or something."

The deputy shook his head. "No. In fact I heard him say one time that he'd better clean his gun some day, because it hadn't been out of his holster in six months—since the last time he'd cleaned it. Fact is, I've seen him in town plenty times when he wasn't even totin' his gun. No, he wasn't one to waste ca'tridges."

Rod laughed suddenly. "You speaking of men always shooting at bottles and signs, reminds me of Everett Bancroft. Now there's a hombre who can really knock 'em off. Couple of weeks back, there were some fellers plugging at bottles in the alley, out back of the Arcanum House. Bancroft was there, watching. He didn't have his own gun, but he borrowed one of the others, and I see him knock off five bottles in a row. Didn't scarcely look like he took aim either. Not that there's a lot of men can't match that sort of thing, but it was the easy way Bancroft did it that impressed me."

75

"I suppose," Quist said absent-mindedly, still examining the gun. He handed it back to Larrabee. "Be sure and keep that safe."

"Naturally." Then, sharply, "Did you get some sort of idea, Greg?"

"I don't know," Quist scowled. "I've got to think about it. Something's clicked in my mind, but I'm not yet sure what it is, either about that gun or something that's been said. I just can't put a finger on it—"

He paused as running footsteps were heard on the sidewalk. A man turned at the office and burst through the doorway. "Rod!" he exclaimed, panting and wide-eyed. "Sheriff Kiernan wants you to once't. He says to hurry. Thought I might find you here—"

"What's up, Sam?" Larrabee demanded.

"I don't know exactly what happened," the man puffed, "but you're to come to the hotel right off. Somebody took a shot at Miss Bancroft!"

Swiftly, Larrabee shoved Callister's six-shooter back in the safe, slammed the door and spun the dial. Then he and Quist started at a fast walk toward the Arcanum House, the man at their heels, stumbling over his own feet in the attempt to keep pace.

VIII

THERE WERE several men near the entrance of the hotel when they arrived, and the lobby was crowded. Larrabee and Quist pushed through to the desk, Larrabee asking, "The sheriff upstairs?"

Nelly Grimes looked somewhat shaken. He nodded. "Gracious, I'm glad your here, Deputy Larrabee. I don't know what the world is coming to. We might all be shot in our beds. Sheriff

Kiernan won't allow anyone upstairs, but I know he'll be glad to see you. And you, Mr. Quist . . ."

The deputy and Quist were already halfway up the flight of steps while Grimes still babbled on. At the top of the stair well, three sides of which were surrounded by a wooden railing waist high, two men stood talking. The doors of Numbers 16 and 17, at the opposite end of the hall from Quist's room, but on the same side, stood partly open; there were lamps burning within.

Sheriff Kiernan moved from his position against the railing, and glanced down. "Oh, you, eh, Rod," he grunted. "I thought more of those snoopy hombres from downstairs were coming—" He paused, his scowling gaze going to Quist at Larrabee's heels. .

"Miss Bancroft hurt bad?" the deputy asked, nodding to the other man.

"Not any," Kiernan replied. "Missed her complete, thank God."

"This is Mr. Quist." Larrabee performed introductions. The sheriff nodded shortly and grunted, "I heard you were here, Quist." The other man was Everett Bancroft. Both were dressed in town clothing, though they wore boots. A narrow-brimmed sombrero covered the sheriff's head; Bancroft didn't wear a hat. The sheriff was a big man with sweeping mustaches, bleached by the sun; he had the beginning of a paunch and his jowls were beginning to droop a little. There was a star pinned to his vest beneath his coat and he wore a string collar and narrow black tie.

Everett Bancroft had good features without being handsome. He had wide shoulders and slim tapering hips. His handclasp was firm and he was more articulate then the sheriff.

Bancroft said, "You sort of slipped in on us, didn't you? We've put two and two together and decided you arrived by stage-coach, though apparently Miss Callister didn't catch your name, at least not all of it. Had a little trouble too, I hear. One of the stablemen—"

Quist cut in, "I had some business carried me up near Wolver-ton."

"My sister and I wanted to welcome you after you had a chance to clean up, but by the time we knocked at your door, you'd gone out." He paused at a question from Quist, then, "No, Helen is all right. Whoever did the shooting fired wide of his mark. She's in her room and will be out here in a minute. Natur-ally, we don't like—"

"Exactly what happened?" Larrabee asked impatiently.

"Some dirty skunk," the sheriff said angrily, "shot through the door at her. No, we ain't the least idea who it was. Nelly Grimes swears nobody come up the stairs, or come down. The way it looks to me, Nelly was dozing at his desk, and the feller sneaked up the stairs, just far enough so's he could push his gun-bar'l through the spokes of this here railing. Then he pulled trigger. Hit the door—"

"Helen and I were both in our rooms at the time," Bancroft explained. "I'm just wondering if it wasn't some drunk. Maybe he stumbled and his gun went off as he struck the floor."

"That's figuring he'd have his gun in his hand when he came up here," Quist commented. "If so, what did he have in mind? If what you say is true, Bancroft, perhaps the gun exploded pre-maturely, somehow, and he got scared off before he could carry out his intentions."

"If that's the case," the sheriff growled, "where did he get to? Everett here heard the shot, and come out instanter. There was nobody to be seen. Nelly Grimes swears nobody passed through the lobby."

Quist swung away from the railing and walked to the door at the front of the hall. The knob turned easily under his hand and he stepped out to the upper gallery. He glanced toward the street below. It wouldn't be much of a drop from here, though there'd be the risk of a man being seen if he dropped to the street

78

with the lights from the hotel shining across the sidewalk.

Quist started along the gallery. There was a step behind him and he turned to see Larrabee in the semi-gloom. "Damn! I should have thought of this," the deputy said disgustedly. "Don't know why Jake didn't figure things this way."

"A man doesn't think of everything all at once," Quist said. He reached the far end of the gallery, just outside his own room, and stopped at the end railing. Adjoining was a flat-topped building of one-story height, with a high false front. A space the width of the gallery extended from the false front to the corner of the hotel building.

"There you are," Quist said. "Whoever did that shooting could have run out here, vaulted over the railing to this roof next door—"

"And dropped off at the rear into the alley back there," the deputy finished.

"Proving it might be wise for me to keep my side window shade lowered," Quist growled. "From the top of this roof anybody could shoot through my window—oh, hell, you see what I mean when I say a man can't think of everything at once. Sometimes I'm just plain dumb. Checking that side window should be second-nature to me."

"I noted you had your front shades drawn."

"A lead slug isn't particular which window it crashes through."

They returned to the doorway into the hotel and found the sheriff and Bancroft looking out. Kiernan said lamely, "I took it for granted that front door would be locked," he said.

"I see what you mean, Greg," Larrabee chuckled, and to the sheriff, "The best of us, Jake, misses things at times."

"That's whatever," Kiernan grunted. "Rod, I want you should take your knife and dig that bullet out of Miss Bancroft's door. Maybe that'll tell us something—no, it didn't go through. You get busy." Larrabee approached the door and started looking for the hole. Kiernan said impatiently, "No, lower. Down near the bottom."

"I'll be danged," the deputy said. " 'Way down there." The bullet hole wasn't more than six inches from the bottom of the door, and about the same distance in from the right jamb, near the hinge side.

"Proving my point," the sheriff said pompously. "The skunk was afraid to come higher up the stairs, so he just come head high and fired through this railing."

"And," Quist put in quietly, "*after* firing he got over his fright, came the rest of the way up the stairs, dashed down this hall and out that door to the gallery?"

The sheriff was suddenly silent. Everett Bancroft chuckled, saying, "I guess you're wrong, Jake. I think my surmise is nearer right, that it was some drunk who stumbled and fell and his gun went off. Considering how low that bullet entered—"

"Where were you, Sheriff, when you got word of this?" Quist asked.

"I don't know if it's any of your business, Quist," Kiernan stated stiffly, "but I was in the Arcanum Bar. Nelly Grimes heard the shot and came after me, but I don't see—"

"Then you probably got through the lobby soon enough to see anybody coming down the stairs, or passing through the lobby. Or perhaps the gunman escaped through the lobby while Grimes was getting you from the bar. That's a possibility of course, but I think the liklier idea is that he left by way of the gallery and the roof next door."

"I know there was no one in the lobby, anyway," the sheriff admitted. "Rod, you going to start cutting out that slug?"

Before Larrabee could reply, the door opened wider and Helen Bancroft appeared. The sheriff stepped quickly forward, sweeping off his hat. "Ah, Miss Bancroft, I hope you've entirely recovered from your fright."

"Nothing to recover from, Sheriff," the woman smiled. "I'll admit I was startled for a moment, but—"

"Helen," Everett Bancroft broke in, "this is Mr. Gregory Quist. Mr. Quist, my sister."

Quist bowed, removing his sombrero. Helen Bancroft put forth her hand. Quist took it and found himself reluctant to release his grasp on the long cool fingers.

Helen Bancroft was tall and slim, with classic features and blond hair, the type known as cornsilk hair; her eyes were very dark as were the eyebrows, her skin smooth and faintly tanned. Her hair was swept back and shoulder length. She wore a dress of some delicate soft material of dark green, with lace at the throat and cuffs. She wore no jewelry of any kind.

She smiled at Quist. "I've heard you lead a rather exciting life, Mr. Quist. One of the stagecoach company men was saying you'd had some trouble on your way here—you and Alex Callister. And now this business. Tell me, do you always manage to arrive when something is happening, or do exciting things just follow and happen when you are settled on the spot?"

"I should say," Quist replied meaningly, "that the most exciting things happen on the spot." His eyes held her for a moment before she glanced away to reply to some remark of the sheriff's.

Larrabee was already down on the floor digging at the hole where the bullet had entered. Everett Bancroft caught at Quist's arm. "Could I speak to you a moment, privately, Mr. Quist?" Quist nodded. Bancroft said, "If you'll step into my room."

He flung wider the door, and stood aside for Quist to enter. The door closed behind the two men. Quist glanced around. It was a room furnished much like his own, but looked more lived in. A Winchester repeating rifle stood in one corner. A holstered six-shooter hung on the clothes rack. A small bookcase held volumes on gunnery and cattle raising, the titles of which Quist read while he was waiting for Bancroft who was busying himself with a bottle and two glasses.

81

"Sit down," Bancroft invited. He held out a glass. "I hope you'll join me."

Quist did. It proved to be excellent bourbon and Quist said so. Bancroft nodded his thanks, adding, "I see you were looking over my books. I'm trying to learn a little more about stock raising. I may decide to go in for ranching. As you probably know, I'm acting as day clerk here at present, more to help out Helen than anything, until I can decide what I want to do. I like this country and may decide to stay."

"I can understand why you wouldn't want to leave your sister right now," Quist said.

"That's the point exactly. And I'm anxious to have the business cleared up. That's why I wrote you, though I had little hope —well, to make a long story short, I was certainly glad when I heard you were here. And all I'd looked forward to was an answer to my letter."

"I answered your letter," Quist said, "but didn't send it."

"You came on instead. Fine. Now I'm going to be frank with you. I'm not a wealthy man—as wealth goes—but whatever your fee—"

"A minute, please, Mr. Bancroft. The letter I wrote was a refusal to your request. You see, I'm under contract to the T.N. & A.S. and can't take an outside job."

Bancroft's brow furrowed. "But then, I don't quite understand. You say you can't help us out—"

"Not directly. You see, my company is anxious to buy the right-of-way—well, you know that, of course. My company thought perhaps I might be able to hurry things up if I came here. Though I'm not sure what I can do. It seems to be a job for the doctors. At any rate, I'm here, on orders from the T.N. & A.S."

Bancroft smiled broadly. "Well, then whatever you discover may be of benefit to us too. I say 'us.' I really mean my sister, Helen. I'm not averse to getting money, y'understand, but after all I can get along all right. Helen acquired a rather heavy debt when she took over this hotel. If it is proved that the money is to come to her, that's fine. If it isn't—well, that's the way the rope sails. Sometimes you catch your critter and sometimes you don't. Right?"

Quist nodded and Bancroft continued, "There's just one thing more. Nobody here knows I wrote asking you to come here. I'd just as soon Helen didn't know about it. You see, she's pretty independent and she's not too enthusiastic about the money she may get. It's not worrying her one way or the other. She likes to feel she can stand on her own two feet. And she wouldn't have wanted me writing to you. So, if you'll just not mention that letter to anybody—"

"Of course. No need to say anything further, Bancroft. I know exactly how you feel, under the circumstances. But you can rest assured you'll get the benefit of any information I happen to turn up—if I do."

They left the room a moment later and returned to the hall. The others looked curiously at them but didn't say anything, beyond Helen's smiling "I hope you enjoyed Everett's bourbon, Mr. Quist."

"A pretty smooth article, Miss Bancroft," Quist laughed.

He turned to Larrabee who was on his feet now, examining the small chunk of lead he held in his hand. "Looks like a thirty-two caliber to me, Greg. What do you think?"

Quist took the bullet, examined it, hefted it in his hand. "I'd say a thirty-two."

"Let me see that slug," Kiernan demanded. It was handed to him. "Small gun, anyway," he pronounced. He slipped it in his pocket. "Didn't reckon anybody around here used pea-shooters," he added disgustedly.

"But they will kill," Bancroft put in. He hadn't asked to see the bullet.

Quist dropped on his knees amid the whittlings Larrabee had

dug from the lower part of the door, and then scratched a match, holding it close to the gouged hole, and with his right ear almost parallel to the floor.

"Detective stuff," the sheriff commented, a certain sneer in the tones.

Quist ignored the remark and got to his feet, blowing out the match. "Luckily, Rod only had to whittle away a half of that hole to get the bullet. The part of the channel that's left shows the course the slug took. Rod, you take a look."

Larrabee got down on the floor and repeated Quist's inspection. He rose, dropping the burned-out match to the floor, and nodded. "The angle that slug took disproves a couple of theories. It wasn't fired by anybody who'd stumbled on the floor; neither was it shot by somebody standing on the stairway and poking his gun through the railing. Not unless the gun was held high above the feller's head."

"And I doubt that's likely," Quist said. "My guess is that, considering the angle at which the bullet entered, the gun was held in a fairly normal position, depending on the man's height, of course, and pointed down. Whoever fired the gun stood just about here . . ."

He crossed to the opposite corner of the hall, taking five quick steps, wheeled and faced the group near Helen Bancroft's door. Then he rejoined the group. Larrabee nodded, "That's how it looks to me."

"Regardless," the sheriff said heavily, "I don't think this is serious. Some drunk like Everett said."

"Somebody fires through Miss Bancroft's door and you don't consider it serious?" Quist asked.

"I didn't mean it that way." The sheriff flushed. "I figure it was just an accident probably. Anyway, I'll keep the bullet. Rod, you look around. Find out who uses a thirty-two caliber and if he was near the hotel tonight. Quist, you don't need to bother any more. As sheriff, I can conduct any investigation necessary."

"It's no bother," Quist said quietly. "Miss Bancroft, I suppose it's useless to ask if you've any idea who did this shooting?"

"I can't think of anyone who would want to shoot me," she replied, frowning slightly. Quist asked if she'd had any trouble with some hotel guest. She shook her head. Quist asked who was staying at the hotel at present. Before she could reply, the sheriff interrupted:

"If you'd been here sooner, Quist, you could have seen them here in this hall. I told 'em to go back to bed and close their doors."

"I imagine," Quist said pleasantly. "I seem to catch the squeaking of partially opened doors every few minutes, so I judge someone is peeking out—" The sounds of three doors being suddenly closed, interrupted Quist's words. Helen Bancroft commented that naturally her guests were curious. She mentioned various guests and the rooms they occupied; none sounded suspicious to Quist. She concluded,

". . . let me see. Hmm. There's a salesmen from the Wickwire Hardware, a stockbuyer from Helmet Packing. Hmm. Number 18 is vacant right now. That honeymoon couple from Wolverton occupies Number 10. Awfully nice youngsters. I'm afraid the bride was a little startled—oh, yes, just across from my room, is the man from your company, Mr. Quist—Mr.—er—Jarrell."

"My company?"

"The lawyer from the T.N. & A.S. legal department. There were two of them here, but the other left this morning."

Quist nodded. "Sure enough. I'd forgotten."

Helen Bancroft's lips twitched. "I think the shot shook him up a little. I was in bed when it happened. I threw on a wrap and heard Everett already out here. I opened my door and Mr. Jarrell was peeking from his room—in fact there were heads peering from doors all along the hall—and I must say he looked rather white."

"No doubt," Quist said dryly. "That shot will likely throw our

85

whole legal department in a dither." He hoped this man named Jarrell was listening behind the door.

They talked a few minutes longer. Quist refused with thanks the offer to partake of more of Everett Bancroft's bourbon, on the plea he wanted to get to bed. Shortly after that the group dissolved and Quist headed for his room and started to undress. Despite a certain weariness, he failed to find sleep at once. Various things kept passing through his mind—Vance Callister's sixshooter, the attempt to stop the stage, the bullet hole in Helen Bancroft's door, Helen, herself, her blond hair and dark eyes. . . .

IX

QUIST BREAKFASTED early the following morning, in the hotel dining room. The lobby was empty when he came through, with neither Grimes nor Everett Bancroft behind the desk. A Mexican girl took his order for pancakes, ham and coffee. There were but three other men at breakfast, one of whom Quist had met the previous night. The other two he judged to be townspeople, probably merchants.

He had nearly completed breakfast when a young fellow in city clothing entered the dining room. He looked about then came directly to Quist's table. "You're Gregory Quist, aren't you?"

Quist glanced up. The man, he couldn't have been more than twenty-one or two, wore a wisp of mustache and a stiff collar. He was pale-complexioned; Quist felt quite sure who he was. "Yes, I'm Quist. I take it you're Jarrell. Sit down."

"Oh, you've heard of me?"—seating himself across from Quist.

"Not much," Quist said shortly. "I noticed you came directly to my table though we'd not met before. You're definitely not local. I guessed you'd done some peeking from your doorway

86

when we were discussing the shooting in the hall last night. You're up early."

The Mexican waitress arrived to take Jarrell's order, then departed. "And so," Quist went on, "I decided you must be one of the company law-sharps."

"Do you think 'law-sharp' is the word to use?"

"Oh, attorney-at-law?" Quist asked politely.

"Exactly. That is, well I'm reading in Mr. Munson J. Nordwall's office, and when I've taken my bar examination I'll—"

"I remember Nordwall," Quist said shortly, "he nearly balled up a job in Dominio for me one time. So you expect to be a full-fledged lawyer—"

"Mr. Nordwall tells me I have a brilliant legal mind. In addition I've the advantage of two years at a very good Eastern university—"

"And in a year or so you'll be running the whole T.N. & A.S. legal department, I suppose."

"Hardly, but I expect to get there."

"Fine. That's going to be tough on Nordwall. Where's he now?"

"He was here until yesterday morning. Then he was called back to the head office. He left me here to keep an eye on things. And that's what I want to talk to you about."

"Shoot away." Quist started rolling a Durham cigarette.

"This shooting last night, at Miss Bancroft. I could scarcely sleep all night. I think you should do something about it."

Quist paused, match flame halfway to his cigarette. "And what do you think I should do, spend my time running around on a search for the man who fired that shot?" He lighted his smoke, and exhaled through his nostrils.

Jarrell flushed. "Not at all. But, as I see it, of paramount importance is the securing of the right-of-way for our company. I'm sure we're agreed on that. It makes no difference either way, whether the Bancrofts or Miss Callister inherit the right to sell it to us. But we must expedite things. As it stands now, a decision is deferred until the fall sitting of court. That is too long to wait—"

The waitress arrived with Jarrell's breakfast. He scarcely noticed it, so intent he was on what he was saying. But Quist had already interrupted:

"Get to it, Jarrell, what do you want?"

Jarrell pointed out solemnly, "Murder was attempted last night. Had it been successful, with Miss Bancroft deceased, the issue would have been entangled that much more. We can't risk that. Now it is my idea—" he repeated—"*my* idea that you get in touch at once with your superior and advise that we not wait for the fall sitting. Suggest—and strongly—that all influence be brought to bear for a special session of the court and that this problem be solved right now. Delay may be costly. I'm writing Mr. Munson this morning—"

"You do that, young fellow." Quist rose from the table. "I don't want to mess in the business. I don't know a thing about the law and any man that tries to play another man's game is a sucker."

"You don't agree?" Jarrell looked dumbfounded.

"I don't agree. Enjoy your pancakes, sonny."

Ignoring the angry look Jarrell shot at him, Quist crossed the dining room floor and stepped into the lobby. Helen Bancroft was behind the desk, bright and sparkling in neat gray. Her smile was warm when they exchanged greetings.

"No worse off for your scare, I see," Quist commented.

"I'll admit that after I got to bed and started thinking about it, I became a trifle shaky," she said. "Your breakfast to your liking?" Quist said it 'hit the spot.' She continued, "I glanced in once and saw you talking to Mr. Jarrell. Isn't he rather young to be representing your legal department?"

Quist chuckled. "He's just sort of an apprentice, you might say. A kind of office boy to write letters regarding what goes on here. Very serious youngster, though. Where's your day clerk this morning?"

"Oh, Everett's not up yet. But there's rarely much doing this early—"

"I notice you're on the job."

"It's my job to be. You can't run a hotel with slipshod methods. Everett's been sort of chafing at the bit. He likes to hunt, but insists the fall is the best time for deer. And he says he doesn't get any enjoyment out of shooting those little Sonora white-tails—"

"I've heard there are a few mountain sheep hereabouts."

"He's been out a couple of times after mountain lion. The stockmen have been having some trouble—"

Sheriff Kiernan's voice interrupted from the doorway leading into the bar. "Mornin', Miss Helen. Mornin', Quist. This too early for you to have a drink with me?"

"I could use an eye-opener," Quist said. He touched fingers to the brim of his Stetson and turned away from the desk.

There were only a couple of other customers in the bar as Quist followed the sheriff to the far end of the long mahogany counter. Quist glanced around. There was an entrance from Main Street and a second pair of swinging doors giving on to Mesquite Street. The bar ran along the inner side of the room. There were a few chairs and tables scattered about.

The bartender set out a bottle and two glasses at the sheriff's order. Drinks were poured. "Regards," the sheriff said.

"Drink hearty." The sheriff's glass was finished at a gulp. Quist merely tasted his.

"I been wanting to speak to you," Kiernan said, drawing out a bandanna to wipe his wide mustaches.

"What I expected when you invited me in here. You've got to admit, Sheriff, you were none too cordial last night."

Kiernan scowled. "Can you expect me to be? Look here, Quist, I've always run Pitahaya County. What I want you to understand, we settle our own affairs 'thout any outside help. Now I can't figure one single solitary reason why you should come here."

They weren't talking loud enough for other customers to hear, and the barkeep was at the farther end. Quist said, "I came here on orders from the T.N. & A.S. I've been asked to investigate. I figure to do what I can. Is that clear?"

"I can't see what there's to do," Kiernan said irritably. "It's practically settled, or it will be when the fall court sets. Actually it don't make any difference who gets that money, Helen Bancroft or Alex Callister, as far as your road's concerned. As next of kin they both have a chance—"

"Who do you figure has the better chance?"

"Helen Bancroft, of course—"

"And you don't like the thought of an investigation that might swing the decision the other way?" Quist cut in.

Kiernan's face darkened. "Look here, Quist. It stands to reason. Both Callister and his wife died instanter. But she had to live the longest to fire the shot." Quist pointed out that Doctor Iverson differed on that score. The sheriff swore. "Iverson's a drunken sot. No man with sense will pay him any attention. So Helen Bancroft is due to inherit and she'll sell the right-of-way to your company. It's practically settled. So why don't you take a hint and leave?"

"What have you got against Alexandra Callister?"

"Sho', I ain't nothing against her. Fine girl. Lot better than her father. That damned—" He stopped suddenly. "That's neither here nor there. Both Miss Helen and Alex Callister has a following in this town. Arguments always breaking out. Now suppose you start snooping around and find something—"

"What?"

"Hell, I don't know"—irritably. "But you might say something to sway public opinion one way or t'other. That could start an argument that might develop into a gunfight. I don't want that. I aim to have peace. So if you'd just go away and—"

"Now, will you have a drink on me, Sheriff?"

"I don't aim to drink with ary man who goes against my judgment," Kiernan stated. "However, if you're willing to pull your freight—"

Quist said curtly, "You've already drunk with a man who opposes your judgment, but at least you don't have to pay for it." He tossed a silver dollar on the bar, spun about and walked through the swinging doors to Main Street, leaving Kiernan staring, slack-jawed after him.

Sunshine shone brightly along Main, making black shadows between buildings. Quite a number of pedestrians were abroad, including several women carrying market baskets, heading in the direction of the general store. Ponies and wagons had started to arrive at hitchracks. A cowhand loped his pony easily along the street and alighted before the post office which was situated in the stage office. It didn't appear to be quite so hot as yesterday, though the day was still young.

"I've decided not to *ever* give you that twenty," a voice spoke at Quist's back.

He swung around to see Alex Callister confronting him, a smile on her face. "Nor my rebate either, I suppose," he laughed.

"After the whizzer you ran on me yesterday, Mr. Quist—"

"I told you my name was Gregory," he said gravely, "and you don't like to be pushed around—"

"I've got a notion to call you Gregory—Greg would be better." She shook her head, laughing. "You certainly took me in."

"It was your own fault. I didn't tell any lies. You just jumped to conclusions. Your new driver must have showed up, all right."

The girl nodded. "Hired a new guard in Charley Biggs' place, too. So you can't have the job."

91

They conversed a few minutes longer. The girl—dressed practically as she had been the day before, though the mannish shirt was of a different color—mentioned the trouble at the hotel the previous night. "Whoever would take a shot at Helen Bancroft?"

"According to the sheriff you and Miss Bancroft both have followers here. Perhaps you may be accused of having something to do with it." He watched the girl narrowly for any reaction.

"That's ridiculous." Alex Callister said promptly. "Actually, Helen and I are good friends—have been, anyway. Of course—" She hesitated. "I don't know how she feels now. We speak when we meet on the street. There is I suppose a certain tension between us."

"That's natural," Quist nodded. He was thinking that Rod Larrabee was wrong: the Bancroft girl was the lovelier of the two, though there was little to choose between them. Likely there was just the matter of one being more mature, more worldly. Alex' head was almost even with his own. A tall girl, no doubt about it. Quist said, "I'd like to get out to the Box-VC this afternoon and look around. How do I get there?"

"I'll show you. I was planning to ride out myself and get some things. It's only eight miles."

"Good. I'll have to arrange at the livery for a horse."

"Look here, why don't you use Dad's horse? One of the boys brought it in one day, and it's over at the stage stable, eating its head off. It needs the exercise." Quist thanked her, and they parted after arranging to meet at the stable at one o'clock.

Quist turned and headed east, hoping to find Rod Larrabee at the sheriff's office. The deputy was just leaving when Quist arrived.

"H'yuh," Larrabee greeted. "I was just heading to get my morning drink and snoop a mite. Join me?"

"I already had a morning drink but I could use a beer to remove the taste from my gizzard." They paused at the edge of the sidewalk.

Quist told him of the conversation with the sheriff. At the conclusion Rod said, "That's the way it would be, I suppose. Jake's getting pretty testy these days."

"You any idea why?" Quist asked.

Larrabee didn't reply. Finally he just shrugged his shoulders. "Let's go get that drink."

They crossed the street diagonally to the Texas Saloon, which stood on the northwest corner of Main and Coyotero Streets, pushed aside the batwing doors and entered. The barroom was cool and scrubbed-looking, the bar running along the right hand wall. Above the back bar the long mirror reflected bottles and pyramided glasses of various sizes. The bartender, a medium-sized man with bald head and curled mustache, and with a white towel tied about his bulging waist, moved up with a greeting to the deputy. There were no other customers at the bar.

"Greg," Larrabee said, "meet Paddy Heinz, half Irish and half German and a renegade from Texas. This is Gregory Quist, Paddy."

They shook hands, and exchanged conversation relative to towns in Texas. Heinz was from Frederickburg and Quist asked if Kurt Ebert's bar was still in operation. Heinz said it was so far as he knew and added, "And I'm no renegade, Mr. Quist. It's just I'm here on missionary work, tryin' to convert some of these Arizona heathen to proper drinkin' habits. With beer to be had they insist on whisky on the hot days."

"A man after my own heart," Quist nodded. They gave their orders. When two bottles of beer had been set out and sampled, Larrabee asked, "Paddy, do you know of anybody around here who totes a thirty-two caliber gun?"

The barkeep considered, shook his head. "I never noticed in particular, but generally they run to heavier armaments. No, I couldn't say."

The deputy thanked him and turned to Quist. "I've covered a lot of ground already this morning. I can't find a thirty-two.

Down at the gunsmith's, Daggert has one for sale, but he's had it in stock for four or five years, with no takers. There and the general stores say they haven't even had a call for thirty-two ca'-tridges they can't remember when—"

The swinging doors parted and a man entered. He was dressed in cowtogs, with a sombrero shoved to the back of his head. A scarred holster, carrying a six-shooter, hung from his belt slanted across the hips. He was swarthy-complexioned with pale blue eyes and his nose showed evidence of a poorly set break at some previous time. There was a sardonic quirk to his thin lips and he had a sort of devil-may-care air.

Quist, seeing the man's reflection in the bar mirror, swung around with his back to the bar. He said quietly, "Hello, Ran-dle."

"Well, if it isn't old Hawkeye himself," Randle said jovially. "Heard you was in town, Mr. Quist. Figured I'd better come around and pay my respects. Judged the Texas bar would be the right place and I wasn't wrong. We Tejanners stick together." He put out one hand and Quist took it, studying the man closely. Randle nodded to Larrabee. "How's it going, Rod?"

"I can't kick," the deputy nodded. "Find a job yet?"

Dodge Randle shook his head. "But I will." He turned back to Quist. "Did you tell our lawman about me?"

Quist said, "I didn't even know you were here."

"I suppose not. You've deflated my pride, Mr. Quist. That goes to show, I'm not so important as I thought I was. How's for a drink?"

"I could use another bottle but I'm buying," Quist said. He motioned Paddy Heinz down the bar. Orders were taken; drinks poured.

Dodge Randle put down his glass, turned to Larrabee. "Mr. Quist and I are old friends. No, let's say acquaintances. More suitable, eh?—" grinning at Quist. "You see, Rod, up in Utah one

94

time I got riding with a bunch of bad boys. We all figured it wasn't smart to work cows for a living—or work of any sort. Mr. Quist didn't agree. He fixed it so I got free board and room for two years, less time off for learning to behave polite to my landlord."

Larrabee said dryly, "I'm surprised you didn't tell me about it when you hit Arcanum City."

"Not me," Randle laughed. "You wouldn't want me to discount my own character, would you? Been behaving myself, haven't I?"

"So far's I know," the deputy replied cautiously.

"Shucks, you don't have to worry about me, Rod. Mr. Quist taught me a lesson. I was wrong and he proved it to me. From now on the strait and narrow road for Dodge Randle."

"How long you been out, Dodge?" Quist asked.

"My landlord gave me a New Year's present. Said I was the modelest boarder he'd ever had. Or maybe he just didn't like horn music." He explained to Quist, "One of the other boarders had left some time before. He give me his slip-horn. Honest to God I learned to play it right well. You ought to hear me play "Rock of Ages" with variations. But some people don't like horn music."

"How come you landed here?" Quist asked.

Randle shrugged. "Somebody was telling me it was good cow country down this way. I needed a job. Wanted to get far away from the old gang—"

"Your pards get out the same time?"

"Two of 'em. The others—" Randle shrugged—"maybe they didn't learn to play their horns well—or whatever they were doing in the orchestra."

The men talked a few minutes longer, then Quist and Larrabee departed, Quist saying, "I'll see you again, Dodge. Behave yourself."

"Nothing else, Mr. Quist," Randle laughed. And added, "Same to you."

Quist and the deputy crossed to the shady side and strolled west on Main Street. Larrabee asked, "What's the story, Greg?"

"Dodge Randle and a gang did some freight heisting up near Salt Lake City—liquor, canned goods—just general freight. I got the proof I needed and a couple of other operatives and myself closed in on them. Randle was the only one that showed brains, despite the fact he had something of a rep as a fast gunslinger. He faced the fact we had 'em cornered. He surrendered, when the rest of the gang wanted to shoot it out. Only for him it could have been a nasty fight. They didn't like it, but they followed Randle's lead. The gang went to the pen."

"He didn't act like he held a grudge against you."

"He didn't show it, anyway, if he did. Probably was a mite nervous about my arrival here. Thought he'd better face up to it right off and learn where he stood. I'll appreciate it, Rod, if you don't tell the sheriff about him—so long as he behaves himself."

Larrabee frowned. "That doesn't make me look very loyal to Jake."

"You're right, of course. Suit yourself," Quist nodded. "Only if he is planning any capers, I'd like to give him enough rope to hang himself, before we stop him. If he's going straight, I don't want to be the one to put anything in his way. You know, give a dog a bad name and nobody wants to hunt with him."

"You feel he's trustworthy then?"

Quist said testily, "Hell, no. I don't know one way or another. How long's he been here?"

"Couple of months I'd say, offhand. I just suddenly noticed him around one day. During calf roundup he got on with Tim Polk's Rocking-P Ranch, but when that was ended, Tim didn't have any more work for him. And none of the other stockmen are hiring this time of year. I do remember Polk mentioning he could give

96

him a recommend as a steady worker, so I guess he's all right in that direction. He filled in at the livery stable when the regular man was laid up for a few days. I never heard anything against Randle."

"Who's he associate with around town?"

"Nobody in particular that I've noticed. He seems to hang with cowhands mostly. Seems friendly with everyone. I don't know, maybe I'd better not say anything to Jake for a spell anyway. Jake might make a big thing of chasing him out of town."

"Suit yourself," Quist said.

"I just happened to think of something. You mentioned Randle's rep as a fast gunslinger. He's right good all right. I told you about the day the fellows were shooting at bottles in the alley. Randle was one of them. Next to Bancroft I'd say he was best."

"Could be," Quist said carelessly. "By the way, I'm riding out to the Box-VC with Miss Callister this afternoon. Any message you'd like me to give her?"

The small man reddened a trifle. "I reckon not." He added, "If she don't know I'm pulling for her, she should."

Quist nodded. They'd reached the corner of Main and Mesquite Streets. Quist said, "I'm going to drift over to the T.N. & A.S. depot, Rod. Just thought of a telegram I want to send."

"I'll see you later then. I've got to keep looking for that thirty-two gun." They parted, Quist turning south toward the station.

X

QUIST HAD his dinner at a small restaurant not far from the hotel, and arrived at the stage stables shortly before one o'clock. Alexandra Callister had already arrived. Her own horse was saddled and waiting; a stableman was just throwing a saddle across the back of a big black gelding, which moved impatiently, as though anxious to be going. Alexandra gestured toward the horse, "There's your mount—" she hesitated—"Gregory."

"Yes, ma'am," Quist said politely. "He looks like quite a horse." He smiled gravely up at her on her pony's back.

"Dad always said he was a man's horse."

"I'll have to prove I can ride him then." Quist moved around to the animal's side and finished the saddling. He placed one booted foot against the horse's ribs and pulled hard on leather, then slightly adjusted the stirrups.

Alexandra laughed, "That'll teach him you don't plan to have that cinch come loose."

A minute later Quist climbed into the saddle. The horse stiffened momentarily. Suddenly its head went down. Savagely, Quist jerked on the rein, yanking the head back with no little force, even before the animal had a chance to buck. That was all there was to it; the horse recognized it had a master in the saddle; there'd be no bucking today. A certain respect showed in the girl's eyes. "Dad always said Blackjack had a tendency to buck when he'd not been ridden for a while."

"You wouldn't warn me ahead of time, would you?" Quist accused.

"I planned to get even for taking me in yesterday," the girl admitted. "I see now you didn't need a warning. Shall we start?"

They rode out of the stagecoach yard and turned west along Main Street, walking the horses side by side. The buildings began to thin out a block past Concho Street, and a few minutes later they crossed a plank bridge over what the girl told Quist was called Rio Bisnaga, adding, "It's not much of a river, except when the rains come. Where it heads up in the Arcanums, it's just a small stream, but it does furnish good water for our holdings all year round." She stopped, "Maybe I should no longer say 'our' holdings."

98

"I would in your place—until things are proved otherwise."

They swung almost due north along the wheel-rutted, hoof-chopped trail, pushing the horses at a steady lope, through a country of bunchy galleta grass and mesquite. Now and then a palo-verde tree waved bright green fronds in the warm breeze. Ahead of them the Arcanum Mountains lifted jagged black peaks against the deep turquoise sky, and across the waving tops of foliage Quist could see stalk-like pitayaha cactus on the rising slopes toward the mountains.

Quist signaled the girl to slow pace after a time. She drew nearer to him, questions in her gray eyes. Quist said easily, "Sort of savage-looking, those mountains. A sort of brooding mystery about them."

Alexandra said, "You're not the first to make that comment. There are tales of ghosts hereabouts."

"I've heard of them. Ever seen one?"

"Not since I was a child. I was always seeing them then, and Dad used to get angry when I tried to tell him so. But there was a lot of blood shed in the old days." She added flatly, "And more recently too."

"What's your opinion of Rod Larrabee?" A sharp change of subject.

The girl glanced at him, looked away. "I think he's a fine peace officer. We used to be good friends."

"Used to? Why not now?"

The girl shrugged trim shoulders. "I don't know. We just don't see much of each other any more. Matter of fact, we quarreled. I don't think it matters to you why." She was silent a moment then the words came with a rush, "Trouble with Rod he's too humble at times. What is called an inferiority feeling of some sort, just because he's not as big as a lot of men. It's crazy, but there it is." She broke off rather hotly, then added, "And that doesn't matter either, Mr. Quist—"

"Gregory—or Greg," he said quietly.

"What does matter," she snapped, "is that you aren't so interested in the mountains or Rod Larrabee, as something else. What do you want? It's not necessary that you beat around the bush. What do you want?"

"I want to ask you some questions, Alex. Answer them or not as you see fit. First, why did your father marry again—a man of his age?"

The girl looked rather surprised. "He'd turned bitter after mother died, years ago. If I'd been a son, it might have been different. But he became hard and relentless as well as bitter. He was arrogant at times, and that made him enemies. Actually I think he was lonely and turned to making money to fill his hours. He'd been in this country a long time, you know. He foresaw that anybody who controlled the approaches to Bisnaga Pass would someday sell at a good price to some railroad. His stage route was doing the work meanwhile, though after railroads came into this country, it didn't pay so well. But he continued running it for a hobby as much as anything."

"Had you had any trouble with him?"

The girl's chin came up. "The past few years we've quarreled more than necessary. He'd ride roughshod over somebody and I'd tell him he was wrong. But he loved me. I know he did. But he was too proud, or stubborn, to admit it when he was wrong. Why he wanted to marry again, I'm not sure. Perhaps a momentary infatuation had something to do with it, or he may have just wanted company. Anyway, he told me one night he was planning to marry Helen Bancroft."

"And you quarreled again? You didn't relish the idea?"

"On the contrary, Greg. Actually, I thought it might be a good thing for him. And I liked Helen. She's pretty much of a woman judged by a man's standards, I suppose. I know there are several men in town who'd be glad of a chance to marry her."

The horses passed through the shade of a big cottonwood

spreading wide branches across the road and again emerged into hot sunlight. The girl went on, "Dad had helped Helen finance the hotel, and she was doing a bang-up job of running it. Efficiency always got his respect, and Helen is very capable. Probably Dad thought they'd make a good team. No, Greg, I didn't oppose the idea."

"What I'd like to know is, why didn't he marry her then? Why did he suddenly turn to her sister, Anne, marry her instead? Do you know?"

The girl considered a moment. "Yes, I know," she said finally. "Is it important? I've never told anyone else."

"It's important," Quist said.

"More false pride, I think, or perhaps he had just fallen in love with Anne. He returned to the ranch one night in a rage, and stated he wasn't going to marry Helen. I never did get the details, but he learned that she had once been some sort of circus performer, or in show business or something of the sort. And Dad just did not like anyone who was in any way connected with what he called 'that sort of an exhibition.' He was narrow minded, I suppose, according to some standards. I tried to make him see things straight, but it wouldn't work. I think his pride was hurt. He always liked to boast of his old Virginia background and family. Even so, I think things might have been patched up, except somehow he felt Helen had deceived him, as she'd told him when she came here she'd beeen running a hotel in Baton Rouge—"

"Where'd he learn about Helen's former life?"

"Anne had inadvertently dropped something and then the story came out. And it wasn't long afterward that he began sparking Anne."

"Inadvertently. Hmmm . . ." They guided the horses around an upthrusting outcrop of granite, then Quist continued. "I wonder. Sisters have been known to double-cross each other. Perhaps she figured that as your father was a good catch, she might as well cut Helen out. You don't happen to know how Helen felt, of course."

Alex shook her head. "I do know she always had a chin-up attitude. She even joked about it one time to me, said something about the shrinking violet always being picked, or something to that effect."

"How did you feel about Anne?"

"I never trusted her. She was just too meek and modest and sweet to be believable. Very pretty, no doubt about it, and just the sort to twist a man around her finger. Dad—I've got to admit it—just went sort of silly about her."

"I take it she hadn't gone in for show business."

"Oh, my gracious, no," Alex said mockingly. "Not Anne. She'd been some sort of governess in a girls' school in St. Louis—so she told Dad. Maybe so. I never believed it."

"Maybe you're biased."

"I'll plead guilty to that too. But she certainly put it on heavy. Handed Dad some sort of story about wanting to bring him something in case anything ever happened to her. She actually persuaded him to let her take out a twenty-thousand-dollar life insurance in his favor." Alex's eyes flashed angrily. "We really did scrap, Dad and I, when I asked him if she was going to pay the premiums. So, from then on I kept my mouth shut. Trouble with Anne," Alex finished savagely, "she was just too damn' sweet to be believable. She even baked cakes and biscuits with her own little hands. Moses on the Mountain! No wonder Dad began to get stomach trouble. But she had no compunction about firing the old Mexican woman who had worked for us for years, and then hiring some young witch who could also act as maid. The girl didn't stay at the ranch, either, after a week of it."

Alex stopped suddenly. Then, "I'd better hold my temper or I'll be accused of killing her instead of her committing suicide. To be brief, after the marriage I just couldn't stay at the ranch. I had some money of my own my mother had left me, so I took a couple of rooms with an old friend of mother's who lives on East Cottonwood Street in town. I spent a little time at the ranch, but mostly in town. Dad didn't like it of course, but we managed a sort of neutrality and I handled stage line business for him."

Quist sat his saddle without saying anything, a deep frown on his face. Again something had clicked in his mind, but he couldn't put finger on it. His subconscious was trying to communicate something to him. Dammit, what was it Alex had said that dovetailed with some other fact. He swore impatiently under his breath.

Alex said, "What's up? Don't you like the way I speak my mind about people? I always have so if you—"

Quist shook his head. "It's not you. I'm grateful for all you've said. I—I guess I was thinking of something else."

They put the horses to a lope once more and before long the wide, far-stretching organ cactus fence that fronted the ranch yard came into view. They could hear the steady clanking of a windmill as they directed the horses through the open gateway and past the big ranch house with its wide shadowed gallery, in the direction of the other buildings forty or fifty yards beyond. At the bunkhouse they drew rein.

XI

STOVEPIPE HUDSON sat on a bench before the combination bunkhouse and mess-shack, just outside his kitchen door, sunning himself and idly peeling a pan of potatoes. With one foot he shoved the pan out of the way from between his feet, and rose, doffing his battered sombrero.

"Hi-yuh, Miss Alex. Yo're a sight for sore eyes."

"It's good to see you, Stovepipe—oh, hello, Joe"—as a tall slim individual appeared at the bunkhouse doorway and also doffed

103

his sombrero. "This is Mr. Quist—Joe Sargent, our—the Box-VC foreman, and Odell Hudson, better known as Stovepipe, who cooks for the outfit."

Quist dismounted and turned to help Alex, who was already on the ground. He shook hands with Sargent and Stovepipe. Sargent was a lean grizzled man with a serious manner and keen eyes, somewhere under forty years. He looked very capable.

"I've got to get a few things at the house, Joe," Alex continued. "Mr. Quist's company sent him to Arcanum City to sort of look into—well, look into things—that is, about the night Dad—died. Likely he'll want to ask some questions. Tell him what you can. Oh, yes, Joe, I've arranged it with the bank. Draw on Holt Traxler for any money needed for the ranch. Where's the rest of the boys?"

The remainder of the crew, it appeared, were out working with stock, shifting some to higher levels. Three of the men were running some freshly broken ponies, teaching them to work under ropes. Sargent concluded, ". . .. and Mizner rode into town this morning to have the blacksmith forge out some new stamp-irons."

Alex nodded. "House is locked, I suppose. I want to get some things. Now that the weather's warming up—" She didn't finish as Sargent handed her a bunch of keys.

"Sheriff said I should keep the house locked. Don't know why, but none of us have been inside—want I should go with you, Alex, or will Mr. Quist go 'long?"

"Neither of you is necessary," the girl said. "I'll not be long. Mr. Quist wants to ask some questions. Take care of the horses will you, Joe?"

She set off toward the rear of the house, while Sargent led the horses down near a corral for unsaddling. Quist dropped on the bench beside Stovepipe Hudson, produced Bull Durham and papers. The two men rolled cigarettes. Gray smoke mingled with blue and was swept away on the soft breeze circulating past the bunkhouse.

Quist said idly, "It was you found the bodies, I understand."

"Yes, sir, and I didn't relish it none either. I just felt it in my bones something was wrong that night."

"Why? What happened."

"Can't say why. I just happen to be one of these fellers feel a calamity before it comes on. I got a gift you might say—"

"And he's always giving it away," cut in Joe Sargent, walking up. The foreman laughed. "Stovepipe is our official prognosticator of evil tidings, you might say—in Stovepipe's opinion."

"Don't be always belittlin', Joe," the cook said defensively. "My maw told me one time I was born with a veil—"

"You'd look plumb cute in a veil." Sargent snickered. "Whatever that is. Long and lacy I suppose. Whoever heard of being born—"

"It wa'n't that kind of a veil." Stovepipe pulled exasperatedly at his straggly mustache. "It's—it's just something I was born with that enables me to know things before they happen. Didn't I say that time when Jugger Malone mounted Anthracite that the hawss would throw him. And it did. And broke his arm. I just knew it in my bones it would happen that time. And when Art Sawyer tooken sick, wa'n't it me that pree-dicted he wouldn't recover—?"

"Yeah," Sargent admitted. "After you heard Doc Forbes say there wasn't any hope for Art."

"That's nothin' to do with it. I just know such things. Like that night Vance and his missus kicked off. It was real spooky all the way along the road. I seen shadows, but they looked just like some of these ghosts hereabouts. There was queer noises. There—"

Quist broke in to ask Sargent, "You were in town that night, weren't you?"

Sargent nodded. "It was payday. The boys like to go in and do a mite of drinking. I generally go along to see they don't over-step and get in trouble. I didn't even hear about Vance and his wife until long after the sheriff and Doc Iverson had started for here."

"How come you returned home early?" Quist asked the cook.

Stovepipe swore. "I hadn't had more'n nine-ten-eleven drinks or so, when the feller that runs the post office found me in Smithy's Saloon where I was doin' a mite of peaceful imbibin'. He's got a letter which same he said was addressed to Vance, but had been put in somebody else's box by mistake. He allows it might be important. I says I'll give it to Vance when I see him, but this post-office hombre says I should take it to Vance right off. We argued that some, and I finally give in, thinkin' maybe it was important and I didn't want to have no more trouble with Vance—"

"You'd had trouble with him that day?" Quist asked.

Stovepipe nodded glumly. "Maybe Vance wasn't real mad at me, but he'd been mighty testy ever since he married that woman —ever since he got mixed with them two women I might say. Anyway, he asks me why I'm drivin' the wagon to town. I tells him I'd run out of Red Dog, and he starts skinnin' my hide off because I don't know how to keep my groceries stocked. Hell, I could of told him I'd run short of flour because his missus was always borrowin' from me, to make him cakes and such, and Gawd knows she wa'n't no cook, judgin' from the baked things I see flung outten the back door and onto the trash pile. But I don't say nothin' about that. I just took my hidin' and kept my mouth shut. But I didn't want no more trouble with him, so that's why I figured I'd better get the letter to him as soon as possible. So I put the rest of the bottle in my pocket, climbed on my wagon and started home—"

"Anybody know what was in the letter?" Quist asked.

Sargent said, "Yeah. Jake Kiernan opened it. It was only a monthly statement from the feed company. Not important nowise."

Urged by Quist, the cook continued. "There ain't nothing much to say about my drive here. I was some sleepy but my nerves was jumpy too. I just felt somethin' was going to happen. Like I say, if you're born with a veil—"

Quist cut in, "See any riders on your way home?"

Stovepipe shook his head. "Now you mention it, I did think once I hear hoofs poundin' off to my left—not on the road—"

"How many horses?" Quist asked.

Stovepipe frowned. "I couldn't tell. Ain't even sure I heard 'em. It was all sort of like a dream."

"Maybe you were asleep on the wagon seat," Sargent put in.

"That I won't deny. I know I dozed off once or twice. Don't even know if I really heard shots or not—"

"Shots?" Quist asked.

Stovepipe nodded. "As I got near the house. Seemed like I heard *one* anyway. But I can't say for sure. But I just felt in my bones there was a tragedy goin' on and I whipped up the hawsses—"

Sargent said, "Stovepipe, you didn't say anything at Doc Iverson's inquest about hearing hoofbeats and shots."

"Why should I? I was under oath, wa'n't I, to tell the truth? And I wa'n't even sure in my own mind. I didn't want to be took up on no pre-jury charge. So I just kept my lips buttoned. A feller I knew once—"

Quist broke in with another question to keep the cook on the track. Little by little, he drew from Stovepipe the account of finding the bodies. ". . . and there they was, deader'n doornails, the both of 'em, and with the gun still in her hand—"

"You're certain they were dead?" Quist pursued.

"Ain't no doubt. I reckon I know a dead man when I see one.

107

Not to mention feelin' of the flesh. There's just something about bein' born with a veil that tells a man—"

"And you left right off?" Quist said quickly.

"Quicker'n scat, Mister Quist."

"You didn't see anybody else around?"

"Everybody except Vance and his wife was away that night," Sargent put in.

"No I didn't see nobody around," Stovepipe said. He paused, frowning. "T'tell the truth, I just don't know."

"You don't know what?" Quist asked.

"We-ell, after I knew they was dead, I figured to get to town pronto. I was sort of backing away and I bumped into the door. That sort of threw a start into me, and I headed for the hall and the back door fast. Then just as I was leavin' I *thought* I heard a noise."

"What sort of a noise?"

"I just can't say." Stovepipe knitted his brows. "It was like a boot or a foot scraped on the floor."

Quist stared at the man, then at Sargent. Sargent said, "It could have been some sort of muscular reaction of a dead body, maybe."

"I tell you they were dead," the cook insisted. "Do muscles move after a man's dead?"

"Sometimes." Quist nodded. "What happened next, Stovepipe?"

"I just saddled up and hit for town soon's I could make it. Headed for Jake Kiernan's office. He wa'n't there. Neither was Rod Larrabee. I asks a feller passin' if he'd seen the sheriff, and he told me he'd seen Jake just a minute before, ridin' near—"

"Riding?" Quist asked.

"On a horse," Stovepipe explained, "a couple of blocks back on Main. That's where I caught up with him. The horse looked like it had been runnin' and Jake looked sort of hot and grumpy. He was just leaving the pony at a tie-rail, when I told him what had happened."

"What did the sheriff do, then?"

"He just sort of looked at me, like I was lyin'. Then his face got kinda of white. Finally he got down from his saddle and made me tell my story all over. It just seemed like he didn't believe me; anyway he didn't seem in any hurry to get movin'. Finally he grabs a feller and sends him runnin' with word that Doc Forbes should meet us at Ziebold's Livery. By the time the feller got back with word that Doc Forbes was out to Uzzell's Rafter-U, havin' a baby with Uzzell's missus, Jake had his own horse saddled and another hired for the doc."

"The horse you saw the sheriff riding wasn't his own?" Quist asked.

"I reckon not. Anyway, he got his own horse at the livery. So there was nothing for us to do but head for Doc Iverson's place, and take the extra hawss with us. Which same we did, after Jake had sent a feller to find Rod Larrabee and tell him what happened. Doc Iverson was sittin' with a half-full bottle and the start of a nice drunk. We finally persuaded him to come to the Box-VC with us. I gotta admit that the ride out sobered Doc Iverson, but, shucks, there was nothing he could do. They was both dead. We loaded the bodies into the wagon, blew out the lamp and headed for the undertaker's. The next day the inquest was held."

Quist asked several questions but could bring out nothing else of importance. "But like I've been saying," Stovepipe continued, "if anybody had asked me, that night, was something goin' to tragedize, I could have said right off, 'yes,' 'cause I just knew. Me bein' born with a veil you might say—"

"Excuse me," Quist said, rising from the bench, "I think I heard Miss Alex call to me. And thanks a lot, Stovepipe. You too, Joe."

"You're welcome if we said anything to help," Sargent said.

"Maybe you did," Quist nodded. "I'll see you later." He started with long strides toward the house, anxious to learn what it would reveal—if anything.

XII

QUIST ASCENDED three steps to a roofed porch. The back door stood open and he pushed on in to find himself in a long hall that reached to the front of the house and ended at a closed door. There were doors giving off the hall on either side. He glanced into the first room to his right; it proved to be the kitchen—heavy iron range, table and chairs, cupboard. Windows at the side and rear walls. Quist raised his voice, "Alex! Where do I find you?"

The girl's head popped through a doorway on the left. "In here—my room—my old room, I should say." He hesitated and she said, "Come on in. I'll be through in a minute."

He passed the first door on the left and entered the second doorway. The girl was on her knees on the floor, stuffing clothing into a large valise. Quist glanced around. It was a girl's room all right, but there were no frills. Bed, couple of easy chairs, a small Navajo rug on the floor, dresser and commode. The girl was placing a couple of framed photographs with the clothing. Quist said, "I just thought I'd get the layout of the house and look around."

"Did you learn anything from Stovepipe?"

"I'm not sure until I think things over," Quist evaded. "I was forced to pretend I heard you calling me, so I could get away from him."

Alex laughed, rose from her knees, brushed a stray lock of auburn hair back from her forehead. In the shaded light of the room, Quist thought, her hair had the tone of copper. He stared at her a moment longer than necessary. Alex saw the admiration in his eyes. "As to the house layout," she said, "the plan is simple. Just a big rectangle facing east with the hall running from front

110

to rear. On the south side are the main room—Anne called it the parlor—the dining room and kitchen. On the north are Dad's bedroom—" she hesitated—"then his office, and this, my room. Back of here is a partitioned space; part storeroom for odds and ends, and part a room for the Mexican woman who worked for us. I'm nearly finished here. Come on, I'll show you through."

They glanced into the dining room, Quist having already seen the kitchen. A doorway led from the dining room into the big main room. Here were comfortable chairs. A pair of deer heads and three framed pictures decorated the walls. There was a book-case jammed with books, magazines and newspapers. The wide oaken table held an oil lamp, a broken spur, a box of cigars, a pencil, and various other miscellaneous odds and end.

Here too Indian rugs adorned the floor of wide planks. Two of the rugs were bloodstained as was the adjacent flooring. Quist noticed the girl's averted gaze. He said quietly, "You don't have to stay with me, y'know."

"I'll stay." Her voice wasn't quite steady. "This is the first time I've come in here, since—since that night."

"You were here that night?"

Alexandra nodded. "I'd been out here early that morning, and then went to town. I left my pony under the *ramada* back of the hotel, where he'd be shaded, as I planned to eat dinner at the hotel. I was feeling furious at something Anne had said that morning. It was foolish of me, but—anyway, I guess I didn't have my wits about me. After dinner I walked to my place on Cotton-wood Street. But usually I leave my pony at the stage stables. However, it just plain slipped my mind. Later that night, a man came asking for me at the house on Cottonwood. He told me about Dad and Anne. I hurried to the stage stables and found my horse there, still saddled. The men had all left some time before. It was only then I remembered I'd left my pony under the hotel *ramada*. Naturally I figured somebody who knew it was my horse had taken it to the stage stables. My mind was too unsettled to give much thought to the matter. I pushed hard and got to the ranch shortly after the sheriff arrived with the doctor and Stove-pipe."

"So you were in this room."

"Not for long. Doctor Iverson told Stovepipe to take me to my own room. Later, when the—the wagon and the men left, I went with them back to Arcanum City."

"But you were in this room. I don't suppose you'd remember whether or not these windows were closed or open?"

"What difference does it make? I suppose they were closed. The nights were fairly chilly a month ago. Wait, I do remember some-thing. I—I didn't want to look toward the floor. I kept my face turned away. And now I remember seeing my reflection in the glass as I walked past the windows. They were closed."

Quist's shoulders slumped a trifle. He drew a long sigh, as though he'd found some disappointment in the girl's story. He raised his head, glanced around, then, "Let's get out of here. You've had enough."

She preceded him back to the hall, pointed to a closed door. "That was Dad's office." They went in, glanced around. A desk, two chairs, a cuspidor on the floor. Quist saw nothing out of the ordinary. He turned to leave. "There's one more room—"

"Dad's bedroom—and hers, I suppose." She led the way to the closed door on the north side of the house, with two windows at the front showing the gallery outside, and one window at the side with the shade drawn. Again, there seemed little to see. Just a double bed, a marble-topped table; a dresser with mirror, a chest of drawers holding an oil lamp and a commode. There was a carpet on the floor.

A sudden exclamation from Alex broke in on Quist's thoughts. The girl sounded angry as she pointed toward the floor. "So that's what became of them. Darn her, anyway—" She suddenly fell

112

silent. "I shouldn't talk that way. She's dead now—the hussy!" She clapped one hand across her mouth.

"What's wrong?" Quist asked.

She indicated two Navajo rugs on the floor, placed on top of the carpet, near the window. "Those are my Two Gray Hills—"

"Two gray hills—?" Quist sounded rather stupid.

"My rugs. They were in my room. Two Gray Hills are just about the finest Navajo rugs made. I intended to take them back with me. And she had to take them."

Quist took a step nearer, scrutinizing the rugs. It was indeed excellent weaving in gray and black. He put his hand to the window shade in the north wall to raise it and get more light on the rugs. To his surprise the shade refused to lift.

"Shade stuck?" Alexandra asked.

Quist didn't reply at once. He said after a minute, "It's tacked tight shut, along the edges, to the window frame."

"What's the idea in that? Jerk it loose, Greg. You can see better. The gallery roof doesn't allow much light through the front windows."

Quist "jerked it loose" and allowed the frayed-edged shade to roll to the top. "No wonder it was fastened tight," he said. "There's no glass in this lower sash. It's been broken out."

"That's odd." Alexandra sounded puzzled. "That doesn't sound like Dad. He was a stickler for getting things fixed the instant they were broken. I'll bet Joe Sargent doesn't know about this."

Quist stuck his head through the empty sash and studied the earth beneath the window. There was a lot of broken glass there, hidden by low shrubs that grew near the foundation of the house. But he had a clear view along a gradually rising incline toward the Arcanum Mountains, broken only by an ancient cottonwood with spreading branches some fifty yards distant. The earth between house and tree had been cleared within the past year, and showed only a spare growth of seedling mesquite, sage and bunch grass rising from the sandy soil.

Speculation ran rife through Quist's mind. He withdrew his head, turned and studied the Navajo rugs on the floor, then said quietly to the girl, "you might as well go finish your packing."

"Why?"—frowning. "What have you learned?"

"Nothing for sure. I just have suspicions—"

"Of what?"

"It may not be nice to see, Alex. You'd best go."

"I'm staying." Lips compressed, chin up.

Quist stooped down and lifted aside the two Navajo rugs. "They needed these small rugs to cover, you see . . . ? A larger rug would have looked out of place on this carpet."

Alexandra uttered a startled exclamation. She said after a moment, "I won't want to take those rugs with me, now. Greg—" a hoarse, terror-stricken whisper—"what's been going on here?"

Each rug had covered a dark brown stain that could have come only from dried blood. Quist re-covered the telltale blotches. He rose, brushed past the girl, turned a key in the front door and opened it, allowing light to sweep into the half gloom of the floor. There were no rugs along the plank floor here, but between Vance Callister's bedroom and the main room, Quist spied three brown drops where they had seeped into the flooring. In the main room, a close scrutiny produced a further scattering of drops, which would have gone unnoticed except for Quist's close examination.

Quist drew a long breath and rose from his inspection. He looked at the girl and saw she was white and biting her lips to keep from giving way. Quist said, "You better go to your room and lie down, Alex. Go on, now, don't be foolish."

The girl forced a wan smile. "I told you once I didn't like to be ordered around. But, Greg, what—?"

"I'm not sure yet," he replied. "I'm going to look around outside. You'd better do as I say, though."

He left the girl standing undecided in the hall and stepped through the front door to the gallery. Making his way around the corner of the house, he stooped to the earth beneath the broken window of the bedroom, and examined the scattered fragments of broken glass. One piece of cracked glass he picked up, showed radiating streaks moving jaggedly from a half-circular opening at one edge. Quist located another section of shattered pane to match it. Now he had the complete circle: a bullet hole of heavy caliber, no doubt about it. He continued picking over the bits of glass, finding further evidence to add to the theory building in his mind.

When Quist returned to the hall, he saw Alexandra just emerging from the kitchen. There was more color in the girl's face now. She gestured toward the several sections of broken glass Quist carried. Her lips twitched slightly, "You going in for collecting old glass, Greg?"

"I want a newspaper to wrap these pieces in."

"In heaven's name why?"

"Maybe—evidence."

"Of what? What sort of evidence?"

"It's not all clear in my mind yet," Quist evaded. "I got to think things over a mite." He followed Alexandra back to the kitchen.

The girl got an old newspaper and string and the sections of broken pane were bundled up, then placed on a table. Quist glanced around, noting various pots and pans and a dishpan of water.

"What the devil you doing?"

"Cleaning up a bit. This kitchen is a mess. That Anne woman was no housekeeper if you ask me. Half the dishes are dirty, and the baking pans. Moses on the Mountain! No wonder Dad had belly-ache."

Quist nodded and said, "I'm going out again. Be back in a short while."

He left Alex, headed back along the hall and outside. Stepping from the gallery, he headed toward the big cottonwood he'd seen from the broken window. Here he started to search the earth looking for 'sign.' There were hoof marks under the tree, but they were far from recent. Also bootmarks that almost went unnoticed, they were so faint. Wind and weather had worked havoc with the prints. Quist worked toward the house, moving in a stooping position. A tiny mesquite seedling, had been stepped on, its trunk broken near the base. A thread from some sort of fabric had caught on one spine of a low-growing prickly pear cactus, the thread now faded. Here and there were other bits of 'sign' that would have been passed over by an unpracticed eye.

Finally Quist straightened up and went back to the house. He locked the front door behind him and went on down the hall to the kitchen.

Alexandra was just hanging up a dish towel. "Well, it's clean anyhow—if I never come back here. What you been doing?"

"Looking around, trying to dovetail a few thoughts. I don't have to ask you that question—"

"That cupboard! Such a jumble. Jars and tins left uncovered. Ants thick in a jelly jar—" She broke off. "I found a small hammer and some tacks. I suppose they're the same as used to fasten that window shade tight."

"Could be," Quist nodded. He didn't appear too interested.

"Greg"—she picked up a small glass jar that might formerly have contained jam or jelly—"what do you suppose this powder is."

Quist took the jar, removed the top and gazed in on the heavy off-white powder it contained. Mixed into the powder were minute crystals of the same color. The jar was about half full.

Quist sniffed at the contents, then dampened slightly the tip of a little finger, picked up a few particles of the powder and tasted them. He put down the jar, went to the back door and spat. Then he returned to the kitchen.

Alex asked, "What did it taste like?"

116

"Not much taste to it. That's why I wanted to get rid of it."

"Have you any idea it's poisonous?"

Quist nodded. "I could be wrong but I think it's ratsbane."

The girl frowned. "We've never had much trouble with rats. There's two cats at the bunkhouse. They prowl all around here. You know, that's not like Dad. He never liked to keep poisons around the house."

Quist said quietly, "Maybe he didn't know it was here."

"Anne must have got it then—" She broke off, unspoken questions in her long-lashed gray eyes.

Quist said meaningly, "Anne Callister did a lot of baking I understand. Your Dad had stomach trouble."

The gray eyes widened, then the tears welled. "You—you mean, she was poisoning Dad—and then—then when the poison didn't work fast enough—she—she grabbed his gun—"

"Now, take it easy." Quist patted her shoulder. She turned, placed her head against his chest. Convulsive sobs shook her body. Quist held her close, speaking soft words. Gradaually the sobbing ceased. Abruptly she moved back, dabbing at her eyes with a small wisp of linen. Self-reproach entered her tones.

"No wonder Dad always regretted not having a son. I'm acting like a cry-baby."

"You've seen too much here, that's the trouble," Quist said.

"But the thought of her—"

"Don't jump to conclusions, Alex," he said sharply. "Get me a newspaper to wrap this jar and we'll get started back. Is your valise closed?"

Ten minutes later Quist and Alex were back in saddles. Quist carried two newspaper-wrapped parcels, the jar of powder bulging one coat pocket. The girl's valise was strapped behind her saddle. Joe Sargent and Stovepipe stood near. Alexandra said, "By the way, Joe, there's a window broken in the side wall of Dad's bedroom. Did you know it?"

Sargent looked surprised. "You don't say. No, I never noticed.

Trouble is, we always follow the road around south of the house —never go round to that side much. I did notice one day that the shade there had been pulled down, but I wasn't close enough to the house to see the window good. I'll send a man to town to get a light of glass for it and—"

"If I were you," Quist suggested, "I'd just take some boards and nail 'em across the opening to the window frame, from the outside. There won't be any rains come for a spell yet. That'll save you going inside. With the court business coming up this fall, you don't want to do anything that might be construed as changing evidence around. Not that you would, but you never know what a lawyer will say."

"Reckon you're right, Mr. Quist." He stood spinning the bunch of keys Alex had returned to him, on one finger.

Quist said gravely to Stovepipe. "I don't suppose you have any more forebodings, have you, Cookie?'

"Well, now, Mr. Quist, I have—feel it in muh bones."

"What exactly?"

"Can't say for certain, just feel there's some trouble ahead. Can't rightly put my finger on it though. That's the trouble with a veil. You see things but you don't see 'em clear. It's sort of like looking through a dirty window or a—a—"

"A veil," Quist completed.

Stovepipe looked surprised. "Danged if you didn't just call the turn," he exclaimed.

Quist and the girl turned their horses toward the trail to Arcanum City. The sun was low now.

XIII

IT WAS after seven when Quist and Alexandra reached town. They left the horses at the stage stables. Quist asked the girl to have supper with him, but after a brief hesitation she refused. He guessed she didn't want to go to the hotel dining room, and could appreciate her reason. "However," she added, "there's a place a couple of doors east of the hotel where I eat occasionally—"

"They have good steaks," Quist nodded. "Rod took me there last night. If it suits you—"

"It suits me. I'll meet you there in half an hour. I can wash up at the stables."

"Fine. I've got to drift over to the railroad depot a minute. See you later."

At the depot he found a reply to the telegram he'd sent that morning. He read it through twice, scowling. It told him little he wanted to know, though a name clicked in his consciousness. Now where had he heard it before? "I've got a mind like a bowl of stew," he told himself disgustedly, and thrust the telegram into his pocket.

From the depot he went to his room in the hotel, quickly washed up and knotted a clean bandanna about his throat. Before leaving, he drew all the shades at the windows and made sure they were locked. The package containing the broken sections of glass he placed beneath his dresser; the bottle of ratsbane he left in his coat pocket.

He descended the stairway to the lobby to receive Nelly Grimes: "Going to have a nice dinner, Mr. Quist? Lovely weather—"

"I hope so," Quist replied and disregarding Grimes' hurt look when he didn't step into the hotel dining room, he passed through the doorway to the street, muttering something that had to do with fussy old maids.

On the sidewalk he almost collided with Rod Larrabee. The two men stopped to talk a few moments. "Knew you'd got back," the deputy was saying. "I saw Alex a few minutes ago."

"Talk to her?"

The small man flushed. "Just saw her pass on the other side of the street. Did you learn anything?"—changing the subject.

119

Quist nodded. "Yes, I've learned—learned a long time ago—that just because a man comes in a package that's slightly smaller than standard, that's no sign he doesn't grade up. I've known a lot of small men who were pure dynamite when it came to a showdown, men I've liked to have at my back. Now you've got to get this idea out of your mind, Rod, that just because you're not so tall as Alex—"

"Aw, now, Greg . . ." In the light from the hotel window the deputy's face was crimson. He didn't say anything for a moment, then went on, "What I started to say, Greg, I found that thirty-two gun—of course I'm not sure it's the same gun that fired into Miss Helen's door—"

"T'hell you say. Who had it?"

"You'll never believe me—Nelly Grimes."

"I'll be damned. Nelly! That little old lady. Tell me."

"This afternoon I was just checking on hombres here and there who might be likely prospects. There was one hombre I suspected. I found him loafing in the hotel lobby. I checked him and found it wasn't him, though he left the lobby right after I talked to him. Then, one of the guests was checking out. He was paying his bill, and Nelly couldn't make the right change. Nelly asked me to step into the barroom and change a twenty-dollar gold-piece. I did and came back with the money. I was leaning on Nelly's desk while he settled the business. Nelly drew out his money drawer beneath the desk—"

"Go on."

"There's a top tray for coins in that drawer, and underneath are bills and papers and so on. When Nelly shoved back that top tray, I saw a small stubby gun in the drawer. Later when the guest had left, Nelly stepped out a minute to wet his whistle—I was surprised he even drank. The lobby was empty. I stepped behind the desk, opened the drawer and got the gun. It was a thirty-two, all right."

"What did you do with it?"

120

"I've got it in my pocket to show you. I haven't even told Jake—"

"Let me have it."

The two men stood away from the light shining from the hotel window, while Larrabee produced a nickel-plated six-shooter with a barrel less than three inches long. Quist took the gun. "It'd make a nice watch-chain charm," he grunted. "Thirty-two, all right. It's clean"—after a few moment's examination. "Full loaded."

"There's been plenty of time to clean it," the small man said.

"Yes, sure. But I can't imagine Nelly Grimes owning a gun, let alone shooting one."

"I suppose he has it to protect his cash drawer. Most hotel clerks have one handy—"

"Let me keep this," Quist suggested. "I'd like a closer look at it." Rod nodded and Quist slipped it into a pocket. Quist went on. "I've got to meet Alex at that restaurant you took me to last night. You might as well eat with us—"

"No, Greg, I—"

"—and as I can't make it for a few minutes yet, you go on in and tell her I'll be along very shortly." Without waiting for a further refusal, Quist turned and walked away, rounding the corner at Mesquite Street. Here he slowed to a saunter, drew out Durham and papers and rolled a smoke and loafed near the side door of the hotel bar. He moved a little farther on, toward the rear of the building where the hotel provided a yard and roofed shelter—the *ramada*—for guests' horses and vehicles. Quist growled impatiently, "I reckon I've played Cupid long enough. Anyway, I'm hungry."

He turned back to Main. He peered through the steamy windows of the restaurant and saw Alex and Rod seated at a corner table. They seemed to be conversing easily enough. They smiled up at him as Quist entered and approached the table. There were several other customers in the place as well.

"I've already ordered steak for you, Greg," Rod said, "though there's time to change the order if you want."

Platters of food eventually arrived. Quist left most of the talking to the girl and Larrabee. He said once, "Alex, did you say anything to Rod about this afternoon?"

"I'm leaving that to you," she replied.

Quist nodded. "I'll give you the story later, Rod. It wouldn't make pleasant conversation. Alex, there's just one question I want to ask, and it won't bother you any. That night you rode out to the ranch, when you'd—well, heard the news, did you make good time?"

"I don't think the sheriff and Doctor Iverson had been there long when I arrived. I really had to work on my pony to keep him going, though. He had a streak of laziness, I guess."

Quist nodded carelessly as though the subject didn't matter. At the conclusion of supper he asked, "Where does Doctor Forbes live? I want to talk to him."

"Over on Cottonwood, not far from where I live," Alex replied. "If you like, you can walk over with me."

"We'll both walk over with you, lady," Quist smiled. Both the girl and Rod colored somewhat, but didn't say anything.

On the street once more, the three turned off of Main at Coyotero Street and turned east once more on Cottonwood, a tree-lined thoroughfare with many frame houses and white picket fences. They walked a block before Rod said, "Across on the corner of Pima, Greg. That house with the light in the bay window. Alex's place is about half a block farther, on this side of the street."

Quist couldn't resist saying, "You know where Alex lives then?"

Neither answered. Quist chuckled, said *"Adios,"* and started diagonally across the street. He looked back once to see the very tall girl and the small man sauntering along. They didn't seem to be in any hurry. "Anyway, I did what I could," Quist told himself.

His knock at the doctor's door was answered by a tall man under middle age with glasses on his nose and a black mustache.

122

Yes, in answer to Quist's question, he was Doctor Vincent Forbes. Quist introduced himself and said he'd like to talk to Forbes a few minutes.

"Oh, yes, Mr. Quist. Come right in. I've heard you were here on the—the Callister business, isn't it?" He ushered Quist into his office. Desk, chairs, medical library; a framed diploma hung on the wall. Through an open door, Quist caught a glimpse of an examination table covered with white oilcloth and a glass case of surgical instruments. The two men sat down.

Quist said, "I understand Vance Callister was a patient of yours." Forbes nodded. Quist continued, "Can you tell me how long you'd been treating him and for what?"

Forbes frowned. "We-ell, it's not customary to talk to outsiders about a patient. I don't suppose, in your case, it matters greatly, though. Roughly I'd say I'd been treating him about three weeks before he died. As to exactly what was wrong with him, I'm not sure. A man of his age, y'know, overemphasizes his ailments sometimes. Again, his years may produce multiple complaints. Vance Callister was a rather testy individual, particularly the times he consulted me. I've a feeling that he didn't get from his marriage what he expected, too. It so often happens—a man of his age marrying a woman so much younger. There's an emotional upset to be considered—"

"Exactly what did he complain of?"

"Burning pains in the abdomen, vomiting, sore throat—one or two other things. Each time he consulted me it seemed to be something different. I prescribed for all ailments, of course. Sometimes he seemed to feel better; at others my medicine didn't appear to produce desired results. But none of it appeared too serious. I had planned to give him a thorough checkup, but I've been so busy—" He broke off. "I suppose you know I'm practically the only doctor in Arcanum City. I'm overburdened. Dr. Iverson isn't well and—"

"So I understand. In your opinion is Iverson correct when he states that Anne Callister died first?"

123

A frown creased Forbes' forehead. "I can give no opinion as to that, Mr. Quist. Dr. Iverson examined the bodies, he conducted the inquest in my absence—as he was capable of doing. I had nothing to do with—"

"Let's forget medical ethics for a minute, Dr. Forbes. What I'm getting at is, is Dr. Iverson mentally responsible in what he says about the Callister deaths—in other words, if he wasn't drunk as a hoot owl would he be capable of knowing what he was talking about?"

A thin smile crossed Forbes' mouth. "I think so—yes. In my opinion Dr. Iverson was a very capable physician until he started to—well, until he became ill, let us say."

They talked a few minutes more regarding Callister's complaints. Then Quist got to his feet. "Thanks a lot, Dr. Forbes."

"I hope I've been of assistance."

"You never know. But thanks anyway. Oh, yes—" Quist paused—"in case it became necessary to exhume the bodies of Callister, and his wife, would it still be possible to determine whether or not Dr. Iverson was correct in his opinion about the time of deaths. There'd be some deterioration of the bodies, wouldn't there?"

"That's probable. Some bodies go faster than others. But I think an exhumation by fall would be all right. At any rate, it wouldn't be up to Iverson's word alone. Other medical men would be called in. I expect to be called. Until the case arises I couldn't say what will be done along those lines. Have you talked to the attorneys for Miss Bancroft and Miss Callister? No? The bank lawyer is handling the Callister girl's interests, I believe. Miss Bancroft's attorney has returned to Tucson for the time being. I've talked to him and he didn't see there was anything to be done until the fall court sets."

Quist thanked the doctor again and a few minutes later was on the street.

XIV

BACK ON Main Street once more, Quist stopped a man and asked the directions to Dr. Iverson's house. The fellow said, "If you're sick, mister, you'd better look up Doc Forbes—"

"I'm not sick. I asked a question."

"You needn't get so snappy. I was just tellin' you for your own good. I don't know for sure where Iverson lives. Out west of town some place in one of those old Mex shacks."

"Thanks." Quist brushed past and walked west on Main Street. Just beyond Concho Street he saw the Lopez Saloon. He entered and found a number of Mexicans strung along the bar. They all turned and greeted him courteously. Quist bought a bottle of beer, drank it and then asked the directions to Iverson's house.

A dozen men came through with the information and in addition assured him that Iverson was the most fine *médico* in all this so *excelente* country, and they hoped that the *señor's enfermedad* was not of the *seriedad*. Quist assured them he wasn't at all ill, and the company beamed. He was invited to drink with them. He drank with them, left enough money to buy a round and then, amid much bowing and genial handshakes, he made his way once more to the street, trying to keep straight in his mind the various directions he had received.

"A fine people, the Mexicans," he mused, as he continued west. "Our own folks could take a lesson in politeness from them."

He strode along until there were no more sidewalks and only winding paths heading off in various directions through a wide stretch of sandy waste and cactus and wind-blown mesquite, seeing here and there in the faint light of the rising moon small Mexican shacks of adobe. There seemed no particular plan to the layout: it was as though the houses had been tossed down helter-skelter by some giant hand. He crossed the tracks of the T.N. &

125

A.S., the rails gleaming faintly in the night and on past a lone pitahaya cactus and a small clump of ocotillo, stumbling over galleta grass and managing to avoid a spiny growth of catclaw.

A sudden odor assailed his nostrils and he eyed a bunched group of shacks distastefully. "I must be on the right track," he mused. "If that isn't Trabuco's goat farm, it smells like it. Now I look for an adobe with geraniums at the front. Seems to me most of these houses have geraniums." He followed the path and within a few moments saw in the pale light a wide patch of geraniums, the red blooms spotted across the patches of green.

The next house was dark. The path swerved to avoid a mesquite tree, then farther on Quist saw a small grove of mesquites, with a house light shining faintly among them. Quist followed the path, stepped on an empty whisky bottle and nearly went down. Moonlight picked out more bottles and tin cans as he neared the house, which proved to be just one more adobe shack looking pretty much like the rest.

Light shone from a window with a rag stuffed into a corner of missing pane. Quist knocked at the door and could feel the peeling paint under his knuckles. Silence greeted the effort. Quist knocked again, louder. From within the house came a scraping of a chair, then further silence. Finally, slurred tones emerged:

"Take your bullet holes or your female complain' to the other doctor. Go 'way. Don' bother me."

"I haven't got either," Quist returned. "I want to see you."

"Tha'—tha's blasted lie. Nobody wan's see ol' Doc Luke."

"I do—my name's Quist."

Silence. Then, "Hear' of—you. Railroad 'tective. Did you bring a—*hic!*—bottle?"

"No. But I can get one if necessary."

" 'S always ne'ssary. C'mon in, Quis'."

Quist pushed open the door, stepped within and closed it again. He found himself in a small room, with a doorway leading into what he judged to be a kitchen. A long cracked mirror hung on

126

one wall, evidence of better days, no doubt, as was the sofa with rumpled blankets, two other chairs and a marble-topped table on which stood an oil lamp with its shade knocked askew, and a half-full bottle of bourbon. Two framed diplomas hung crooked on a wall, one of which Quist was to learn later had been granted by a European university.

Iverson sat slumped in a worn easy chair beside the table, an empty glass clutched in one hanging hand. He was a spare man, grizzled, with a mop of iron-gray hair combed straight back, though wisps of it kept falling over his forehead at every moment. There was a ragged beard of the same shade. Despite their bloodshot, bleary aspect, the eyes were intelligent.

Quist advanced farther into the room. Without rising, Iverson looked groggily up at him. "Pour yourself drink an' siddown," he mumbled. With an effort he shifted in his chair and pointed a waggling forefinger in the direction of the kitchen. "Fin' a glass out there. We get your—*hic!*—bottle, when this one's—gone, Misser Quis'."

"I'll pass up a drink right now, Doctor Iverson. I want to—"

"Pash up a—*hic!*—drink?" Iverson sounded hurt. "Don' ever pash up—*hic!*—drink. I'm jus' star'ing in."

Quist thought, And you sure have a lovely start. He said, "I want to talk to you a mite." He drew up a chair near the table.

"Abou' what?"

"This business of the two Callisters' deaths—"

"Oh, no, you don't." He looked owlishly at Quist. "I don't inten' get start' thash 'gain. I tried my bes' make people unnerstan' Anne Cal'ster died firs'. You know wha'? They jus'—*hic!*—laughed at me. I'm jus' drunken ol' Doc Ive'son. Nobody wan's lissen t'me."

"I'm very anxious to listen to you," Quist said.

Iverson's lids dropped, slowly raised, trying to focus on Quist's features. "Jus' can' believe it," he hiccoughed. "No—I refuse say anyzing more on the subjec'."

127

"You figure Alex Callister hasn't any right to her father's money?"

A trace of belligerence crept into Iverson's tones. "You got no righ' say that. Alex—fine girl. I brought her—into thish worl'. Should be her—*hic!*—money. But—nozzing I can do—'bout it."

Quist pretended anger. "Did you or did you not," he snapped, "when you took your Hippocratic oath, promise to do all possible to aid humanity through your profession?"

Iverson's already flushed face became even redder. He straightened a little in his chair. "I've done nothing—to violate—that oath. I—"

"Think it over," Quist said sharply. "Sure, I know, I've heard about you. You lost your wife and your home. You turned bitter. You've quit on the job. Doctor Forbes has more than he can handle. I'm sure he'd appreciate your taking part of the business." Quist was cursing himself for a dirty-dog even while he talked. "Do you suppose your wife would want anything like this—?"

"Now, Quis', I won' lissen to nozzer word—" He started to rise from his chair, then sank back.

"You'll listen all right," Quist rushed on, "unless you want folks to continue to think you're just a drunken old soak. All right, you've had some tough luck. Naturally your practice went to pieces when Forbes came in. You weren't tending to what you had, and Forbes started to take over. He was new. The new broom always sweeps clean, but what a lot of people don't understand is that it raises a lot of dust too—dust that gets into their eyes and makes them forget what a great doctor they already have here."

Iverson's head sunk lower. He considered his empty glass, started to reach for the bottle, then let his hand drop again. He drew a long sigh, wiped his mouth with the back of one hand. With an effort, he raised his bloodshot eyes to Quist. "Ask what you wan'," he said in a weary voice, "I'll tell you wha' you wanna know."

"Good. But you're in no condition to talk right now. First, have you anything in your medicine chest that will sober you up—fast?"

A trace of a smile twitched at Iverson's lips. "Not as fash—fast"—with an effort—"as you want. But perhaps . . ."

"Go take it," Quist ordered.

It was a struggle to get out of the chair, but Iverson made it. He staggered across the room. Quist heard him fumbling about at an old chest of drawers, then the man made his rocky way to the kitchen, where Quist hoped the drinking sounds he heard had nothing to do with whisky. A moment later the kitchen door slammed.

Quist went to the kitchen, struck a light and lighted an oil lamp in a reflecting hanger on one wall. He found some kindling in a box and built up a fire in the sheet-iron stove. Water for a coffee pot was found in a pail. There was coffee in a can. Iverson hadn't returned. Quist listened and heard him being sick outside.

Quist returned to the front room and drew the window shades to the bottom. What had happened before might happen again. He studied the broken mirror on the wall, then considered a window on the opposite side of the room. His lips tightened a little.

It was some time before Iverson returned. He looked pale and shaken. He spied the steaming black coffee on the marble-top table and sent Quist a grateful glance. He sank into his chair and reached for the cup, but his hand was too shaky to hold it. He set it back on the saucer.

Quist smiled. "And now I'll prescribe for you, Doctor." He indicated the extra glass he had brought in. "And at the same time join you in that drink." He poured two glasses, set one on the table.

Iverson looked longingly at the glass, then slowly shook his head. "I'm quitting," he announced.

"You're trying to do it the hard way," Quist said. "The way to swear off isn't through definite statements like that. The best way is to feel you can take a drink any time you like and then control it for the time being and not take it. Eventually you'll be able to enjoy your drinks. You can't tell me it's any fun what you've been doing." Iverson shuddered. Quist went on, "Whisky makes a mighty good medicine sometimes. I'm your doctor for the moment." Again he extended his glass. Iverson downed it, made a wry face, shuddered.

After a time his hand was steady enough to hold the coffee cup. When it was finished, Quist poured more coffee. There was no more whisky. Something over an hour later, Quist judged him ready to talk. "One thing you've done by letting people get you down," he said, "is encourage Alex Callister's enemies." Iverson looked puzzled. Quist explained, "You claim Anne Callister died before her husband did. There's one enemy who'd like to shut you up."

"Can you name him?"

Quist shook his head. "I couldn't say for sure. The man I mean is the one who took a shot at you a few nights back, through your window. Was your window open that night?"

"I'd opened it that day and forgot to close it." He smiled, "I was keeping warm on *Old Crow*. But I never felt that was intentional —just somebody's wild bullet—"

"Get that idea out of your head and keep your shades down from now on."

"But—but the bullet didn't even come near me. It went through that mirror—"

"I know. I've been thinking things over. It was night. There's a lot of mesquite growing around your house. The view wasn't too clear. Your lamp is shaded. I think the fellow saw your reflection in the glass and thinking it was you, let fly."

Iverson's jaw sagged. "It might be. I had just started out to the kitchen—Mr. Quist, you could be right; consider the angle from the window to the mirror and where I was passing—"

Quist cut in, "As I say, keep your shades drawn nights." He changed the subject. "Doctor, if a patient came to you complaining of burning pains in the abdomen, vomiting, nausea, sore throat, being thirsty all the time, what would you prescribe?"

Iverson considered. "I might suspect poisoning. I remember one time a cowhand at the Star-Cross came to me with those symptoms and a few others"—Iverson named them. "In the absence of the cook he'd mixed some biscuits for himself and got the cook's baking powder confused with a jar of ratsbane the cook kept nearby."

Quist produced from his pocket the jar of white powder, and handed it across. The doctor tested the powder as Quist had earlier that day, spat and then took a drink of coffee. "Arsenic trioxide," he pronounced, "better known around here as ratsbane. Where did you get this?"

Quist told him, adding, "Anne Callister was always baking cakes and such. Shortly after Callister married her he complained of the symptoms I've mentioned. Dr. Forbes treated him, but evidently didn't know what was wrong—"

"Forbes is a good doctor," Iverson interrupted. "He's not been out from the East long enough to know ratsbane is easily procurable out here. Neither has he had the experience I've had. And, as you said, he's overworked. I intend to do something about that, too—" He broke off, then, "But, good Lord, Quist, are you saying Anne Callister was trying to poison her husband to death, and when he didn't die fast enough, she shot him?"

"It's beginning to look to me as though she had the idea of poisoning him. Taking it slowly, maybe, so no one would suspect, rather than give him a deadly dose all at once."

"Why then, should she commit suicide after she shot him?"

"I'm not giving you my reasons right now, but I don't think

131

he was murdered by his wife. Neither do I think she committed suicide—no, wait, I'm not ready to explain yet."

Iverson's eyes were wide. "I'll be damned!" he exclaimed.

"I'll give reasons for telling you this when I've everything sewed up to my liking. Meanwhile I'm asking you to keep quiet about things. And now I'd like to know just what makes you think Anne Callister was dead before her husband, assuming they were killed by some third person, within minutes of each other. I understand that death was instantaneous in both cases."

"Instantaneous is a relative term, Mr. Quist, in my opinion. A person may become unconscious at once, when a fatal bullet enters his body, or through some other mishap, but I do not believe he dies instantly. Crippled organs may strive to carry on, despite wounding, and thus a man may take anywhere from two or three minutes to ten—maybe longer—to succumb, if hit fatally. In the case of any man or woman, it is my belief that if they each received identical lethal wounds, at the same instant, the man would be inclined to live the longer. Men are stronger physically than women—tougher muscles, bones, tissue; a man would be able to withstand better the shock of such a shooting. If I had to give odds in such a situation, I'd give them on the strong possibility of the man lasting the longer—if only by seconds."

"Callister and his wife didn't receive identical wounds, of course—or did they?"

"Let's say the bullets took somewhat different courses after entering the body, though the positions at which they entered weren't too far apart. In Anne Callister's case, the bullet missed the sternum—"

"She was shot in front," Quist pointed out.

"The sternum is the breast bone," Iverson explained. "After passing the sternum, the bullet struck the upper edge of a rib, which deflected it on, upward, and threw it sidewise, until it perforated the aorta. It then followed a back rib around and lodged against a vertebra, bringing about a fracture which contused the spinal cord—"

"Whoa!" Quist looked a bit bewildered. "Let's get less technical. You've lost me. I don't even know what an aorta is—"

"Put it this way. The bullet passed between two ribs, ranged upward and cut the aorta. Then it came to rest against the backbone. Cutting the aorta alone did the job."

"Fast?"

"The aorta is a vessel that carries the blood from the heart. Cut, it fails to function. Therefore, no blood for the body. No blood, no life, the end! Yes, quite fast. Offhand I'd say within two or three minutes. Maybe less and *maybe* longer. In the case of a woman, I doubt it would be longer."

Quist looked thoughtful. "Call it three minutes, so we'll get a figure to work with. What about Vance Callister's wound?"

"There again," the doctor said, "the bullet passed between ribs, but it wasn't deflected as in Anne Callister's case. Instead it ploughed right on, struck the ventricles—there was considerable laceration of the heart—"

"Ventricles?" Quist interrupted, frowning.

"*Umm* . . . let me see. Put it this way: the ventricles are simply chambers through which the blood passes on its way to the arteries. Clear?" Quist nodded, and Iverson continued, "The laceration of the heart brought about a hemorrhaging through the pericardium and—"

Quist raised one hand. "Help!"

Iverson raised his eyebrows. "Pericardium? The pericardium, to put it simply, is just a casing, or sac, about the heart. With that ruptured, the blood flowed into the left chest cavity, thus lessening the pressure in the pericardial sac. That brings death, of course, but not so quickly as in Anne Callister's case. I've known men to linger around fifteen minutes, even though unconscious, under a similar wound; I had one patient who lasted over an hour. In my experience I'd say a good average would be around eight to ten minutes."

"Make it eight, for another figure to work on. You examined those bodies pretty thoroughly, didn't you?"

"I started on them that same night, at the undertaker's. Followed the course of the forty-four bullet in each case. A forty-four can create a lot of damage—"

"You're certain they were forty-fours, doctor?"

"Absolutely. To make certain I weighed 'em on my small scales. The one from the woman's body was battered somewhat, but even without the weighing, I felt sure it was a forty-four. I was as thorough as I knew how to be. By the time I finished with the two bodies, it was broad daylight. I grabbed a couple of hours' sleep and managed to stay sober until after the inquest. Made sure the coroner's jury didn't get a drunken man's muddled opinion."

"Both bullets entered pretty straight in, didn't they?"

"I don't know how, but you guessed right. Only a slight angle showed. If you've ever noticed, a bullet wound in the body is a roughly circular wound, a bit ragged around the edges of course. Circling these edges is a small brownish-red rim of abrasion. A bullet entering on an oblique leaves a wider rim on the side of the hole the bullet comes from. In the case of the two wounds I examined, the abrasion was quite uniform. The shots may have come from a *slightly* lower level."

"And I feel quite sure there were no powder burns on the clothing," Quist pursued.

"I saw none," Iverson stated. He continued, "With the jury's verdict in, I got a bottle and relaxed. As a matter of fact I practically blanked out for several days. It was only after I had heard of the contents of the Callister will that I gave an opinion that Anne Callister had been first to die—and did that start trouble!" He paused. "I just happened to think that if those bodies have to be exhumed, that arsenic has a habit of slowing the deterioration of a body to some extent. I hope to have my opinion verified by one or more reputable medical men."

"You've convinced me the woman died first, without any other opinions."

The doctor didn't reply for a moment, then he said dryly, "I think you've convinced me of one or two things, too, Mr. Quist."

Quist glanced at his watch, just before leaving the doctor's house. It was two in the morning. As he wended his way back toward town, following the broken paths through mesquite and cactus, he mused: "Sobering a drunk takes time, but it was worth it. First, I play Cupid. Now, maybe, I'd better join the White Ribbon Temperance Society."

XV

THERE WERE but few lights shining on Main Street by the time Quist returned to the center of town. One or two bars showed yellow rectangles at their windows, including the hotel bar. A faint light shone from the hotel lobby. Quist passed but one pedestrian on his way to the T.N. & A.S. station. The moon was high now, though obscured now and then by drifting clouds.

The sleepy-eyed station-master-telegrapher read the credentials offered. His eyes widened. Quist asked for an envelope and a few sheets of paper, retired to a bench at one side of the depot, and wrote a letter to Jay Fletcher, requesting certain information. He concluded:

". . . I know this sounds like a large order, Jay, but fast action may save further killing. Get every possible operative on it, and any other contacts necessary. I want full information

135

on the names given above. Send it by train conductor, in a
sealed envelope, to this station. I figure our man, here, is all
right, but sometimes telegraphers do talk too much, without
meaning to. And I want everything kept as secret as possible,
until I conclude the time is right to act. Yours in a hurry,

Gregory Quist."

He sealed the envelope a bare three minutes before the eastbound Limited came thundering up for its brief halt at Arcanum
City. No passengers alighted or got on the train. The depot was
practically deserted. Through swirling smoke and steam from
the panting locomotive up ahead, Quist sought out the conductor, when the man had finished talking to the station master.
Again, Quist produced his credentials and told the conductor
what was wanted.

"When you've finished your run, give this to the conductor on
the next stretch. Make it clear that this letter is to reach Jay
Fletcher, in El Paso, with no delay. Actually it's a life-or-death
matter. Jay should be in his office when this letter gets there, but
if he isn't, reach him at his home."

The conductor nodded understandingly. There were no useless questions, and a moment later the train roared off into the
night.

There was no one in the bar when Quist reached the hotel. He
stopped for a bottle of beer and then passed through into the
lobby, where the dozing Nelly Grimes straightened in his chair
behind the desk. "You're returning late, Mr. Quist," he said
primly.

"I'm sorry, Mr. Grimes. I know it's 'way past my bedtime. I'll
try not to let it happen again."

"Something important no doubt," the night clerk fished.

"I was sitting up with a sick friend."

"Deputy Larrabee has been asking for you all through the
evening." The clerk handed across the key to Quist's room.

136

"Thanks. I'll see Larrabee in the morning. Good night."

He ascended the stairway from the lobby to the upper hall, feeling that he was followed by disapproving eyes. The ceiling lamp overhead burned low. He rounded the railing about the stairwell, passed the other closed doors, and inserted the key in his door lock.

Quist turned the key in the lock, withdrew it, dropped it into one coat pocket. He turned the knob then abruptly slammed the door inward, where it met a sudden resistance. Someone was waiting behind the door! Quist leaped into the darkened room, whirled to one side, the forty-four Colt flashing from beneath his coat.

"Hold it—!" he commenced, then went crashing over a chair to sprawl awkwardly on the floor, his head striking against one bedpost as he went down. The blow stunned him momentarily. His gun went flying from his hand.

A six-shooter slammed through the gloom, flashing orange light in the room, directed at the point where Quist had stood but an instant before. Then the unknown man made a dash for the hall, jerking the door closed behind him.

Struggling to hands and knees, mind clouded, Quist managed to climb erect. He heard running steps in the hall. Quist's head cleared. He jerked open his door and saw a big man frantically pulling at the door leading out to the upper gallery. The door swung back and Quist's assailant started through. From his own doorway, Quist made a flying tackle, arms closing about the knees of his opponent. Both men crashed down, then struggled up, the big man chopping awkwardly with his gun barrel at Quist's head, in an effort to break loose and bring the muzzle to bear. Quist blocked the blows, seized the man's right wrist, bending it back sharply. At the same instant he swung his fist to the big man's jaw.

The gun exploded toward the ceiling as the man staggered back through the doorway and out across the gallery, arms flailing futilely. There came the sudden, sharp cracking of splintered wood as the gallery railing gave way under the violent impact of the big man's plunging weight. A brief moment he seemed to be suspended motionless in space before he vanished over the edge and fell with a heavy crash to the sidewalk below.

Only then did Quist hear Larrabee's voice at his shoulder, as he moved to the edge of the gallery looking beyond the splintered railing to the still form huddled on the planks below. The deputy spoke again, "Greg, what in God's name happened?" Quist was already heading for the stairway, Larrabee close behind. A couple of doors opened cautiously; voices were heard in the rooms. Somewhere, outside, a man's excited voice sounded along the street.

Quist said bitterly, "I outsmarted myself I reckon. When I left my room earlier this evening, I left the light turned low. When I opened my door a couple of minutes back, the room was dark. I figured somebody was waiting behind the door. I slammed it back hard, jumped into the room and grabbed my gun. And that's when I stumbled over a chair and went down. Struck my head; made me groggy for a minute. The feller ran for it and opened the door to the gallery. I'd dropped my gun and had to dive for him. We struggled a minute, before I managed to clip him on the jaw. He hit the railing and dropped."

By this time they'd reached the lobby. Nelly Grimes, white-faced, started to bleat incoherencies. Neither man paid him any attention. Quist jerked open the door to the street. A group of wide-eyed men had gathered about the still form on the sidewalk. Everyone talked excitedly. Larrabee dropped to one knee by the side of the prone man, turned him on his back. Light from the lobby shone across the form of a shabbily dressed, pallid-faced bewhiskered giant of a man. He was unconscious, breathing faintly. His eyes looked glazed. His head had wobbled when Larrabee moved him. The deputy said, glancing up at Quist, "It's Hunk Worden."

138

"Who's Hunk Worden?"

Larrabee didn't reply at once. He spoke to the men standing near, "One of you hombres run over to Doc Forbes. Get him back here on the double. I think Worden is finished, but . . ." Two men took off in the direction of Cottonwood Street. One fell behind and returned. The other ran on. Larrabee answered Quist's question: "Can't exactly say who Worden is. He's just one of the hangers-on in town. I've jailed him a couple of times for being drunk. He's a powerful brute, but I've rarely seen him do any work."

"Who are his pals?"

"I don't know of anybody in particular." He looked at Worden again. "I don't think this hombre is going to last long. His head acted like he'd broken his neck, when he hit." Larrabee rose to his feet.

"That's what I thought," Quist nodded. He indicated Worden's sombrero, some distance from the sidewalk, in the street. "It took a jolt to knock that hat off. It's my guess his neck struck that tie-rail bar. With all that weight he carried. . . ."

"Looks damn' possible." The deputy frowned. "I'd like to place something under his head, but if it's his neck I hate to move him again." Worden's eyes were half open now, but there was no sign of life in him. Blood trickled from one corner of his mouth.

More men were gathered before the hotel now. Quist asked, "How come you got here so fast, Rod?"

"Didn't see you all evening. Wondered where you were. Knew you were going to see Forbes. Went there. He didn't know where you went. I asked in saloons around town, coming back here now and then, to ask Nelly if you were in. Finally tried that Mex Saloon, beyond Concho. Heard there you'd gone to Doc Iverson's place. I walked out there. It was all dark. Figured Doc was sleeping off a drunk. Came back here. Nelly said you'd just come in. I'd just started up the stairway, when I heard the shot. Worden was just starting down, when he saw me. He wheeled

139

and ran back. I got to the second floor just in time to see you slug him out across the gallery—"

"What in the devil's happened?" a new voice broke in.

Quist turned and saw Everett Bancroft at his shoulder. Bancroft's hair was tousled; he'd pull his trousers on over his nightshirt. Quist told what had happened. Bancroft frowned. "What was the idea? Did he figure to rob you, or what? You ever have trouble with him, Mr. Quist?"

"Never saw him before," Quist said. "I don't know what was back of it."

"This shooting keeps on," Bancroft said uneasily, "Helen's hotel will be getting a bad rep. I guess I'd better go tell her about it. She's having cat-fits upstairs." He lingered a minute longer. "I'm surprised the sheriff isn't here."

Larrabee said, "I doubt Jake even heard the shot down to his boardinghouse. Unless someone tells him—" He broke off as he spied Dr. Forbes approaching, black bag in hand. Forbes appeared to have dressed hastily. He opened the bag, knelt at Worden's side and started his examination. After a minute he closed the bag and got to his feet.

"I might as well have stayed in bed," he said shortly.

"Dead?" Larrabee said.

"Dead. Neck's broken. Maybe other injuries as well. Can't say without further examination which I see no use of making. Get him to the undertaker's. Rod, will you round up a coroner's jury for me? Inquest tomorrow afternoon—let me see—make it three-thirty."

With the help of a couple of other men, Larrabee carried Worden's body to the undertaker's establishment which was situated in the next block, on the south side of Main.

The small crowd began to disperse. Forbes strode off down the street. Quist returned to the lobby of the hotel. "This—this is a terrible thing, Mr. Quist," Nelly Grimes quavered. "Imagine, right in the Arcanum House. Mr. Bancroft was saying—"

140

"How many keys are there to my room, Grimes?" Quist cut in.

"What? Oh! There are two keys to each room. We—"

"You didn't give my other key out by mistake?"

"Certainly not, Mr. Quist." He turned. "It's right in your box as it should be. You have the other one I suppose."

"Is there a master key to fit all doors?"

"I have one in my desk drawer, but it's not been used—well, since I've been here." His gaze avoided Quist's.

"How long is that?"

"Miss Helen hired me shortly after she bought this hotel."

Quist thanked him and went on up the stairway. In the upper hall he was met by Helen and Everett Bancroft. Helen Bancroft immediately offered apologies for what had happened. Quist told her to forget it. She went on, "It's very kind of you to take it that way, Mr. Quist. Somehow, you always seem to catch me at the wrong time—I—well—I seem to have to dress hastily, and—and—"

Quist looked at her, holding her eyes a moment. She had on a colorful wrapper and a dark scarf covered her blond hair. "It seems my good fortune to catch you at such moments," he smiled. Helen Bancroft colored under his gaze, but before she could say anything, Everett Bancroft interrupted:

"We've been waiting for you to come upstairs. Helen and I would like to inspect your room and see that everything is all right."

"Of course." Quist led the way to his room and lighted the lamp. He reached down and righted the chair over which he'd fallen. "I took a spill over this when I came in. Likely saved my life, though, as Worden's shot went high overhead." He explained what had happened to the Bancrofts, the woman's eyes widening nervously. "So I got out of it with a bump on the head," Quist concluded. He felt gingerly the growing lump at the right side of his head, near the top. "I—"

"What gets me," Bancroft put in, "is how the man entered your room. I've questioned Grimes closely. He swears no extra key has been out, of his possession. Of course, this is an old building. I'd not be surprised if one key, with a little manipulation, would open any of these doors. Helen, you ought to have new locks installed." Before Helen Bancroft could answer, Bancroft said, "Look here."

He strode quickly across the room to a front window with a sort of rumpled shade, drawn to the bottom. "This looks—" He broke off, raised the shade. "Here's the answer, Mr. Quist. Somebody forced the window lock."

Quist and Helen moved nearer, Quist conscious of the heady perfume of her presence. The lock had been forced, all right. The lock hung loosely by its screws; the wood was splintered. "You called it, Bancroft," Quist nodded. "So I guess the hotel keys are all right."

"But, what was Worden's object—?" Helen Bancroft began.

"Worden likely figured to rob you," Bancroft interrupted.

Quist voiced no reason for Worden's action. The three talked a few minutes longer, then the Bancrofts headed for their rooms. Quist went to the wash-basin and started bathing the lump on his head. There was a knock on the door. Quist stooped and got the six-shooter he'd dropped, then said, "Come in." He shoved the gun beneath his coat when Rod Larrabee entered and closed the door.

"I won't keep you a minute, Greg," the deputy said. "There's just this—it didn't mean anything before, but now maybe it does —I saw Dodge Randall talking to Hank Worden earlier in the evening. I saw him give Worden some money. Why, I don't know. There was a hundred dollars in Worden's pockets when I went through his clothing at the undertaker's. Anyway, maybe it's something to think about."

Quist nodded. "I'll think about it."

"I don't suppose you've learned anything new."

"Maybe." Quist went to the window with the broken lock, raised the shade. "Do you suppose Worden got in this way?"

Larrabee studied the broken lock, the splintered wood. "It's been forced, Greg. Chisel, maybe. Still—I don't know"—frowning—"this is wrong. It looks to me as though it might have been forced from the inside. You can see tool marks—"

"Yes." Quist smiled thinly. "The way it looked to me too. I likely wasn't supposed to examine this too closely, and it was meant to fool me. It doesn't. And I don't think Worden intended to shoot and arouse the hotel either. I figure he just intended to hit me over the head, and finish me more quietly—a knife maybe—later. And there's something else. When I stooped to get my gun from the floor, I noticed that a package I'd placed beneath the dresser was gone. Certainly, Worden didn't take it with him. The Bancrofts just left here, and they didn't have it with them."

"Perhaps Worden had already tossed the package to somebody on the street before you arrived. What sort of package was it?"

"Broken glass, wrapped in a newspaper. It's gone."

"Broken glass?"

"Something I picked up at the Box-VC this afternoon—now, I guess, it was yesterday afternoon—when I went there with Alex Callister. Sit down, I'm going to bring you up to date on a few things. It won't take long, because I want to hit the hay. But there's this for you to think about—instead of a murder and a suicide at the ranch that night, there was a double murder."

XVI

QUIST SLEPT LATE the following morning, and it was after nine o'clock when he emerged from the hotel dining room. Everett Bancroft was behind the desk in the lobby when Quist came through, after breakfast. The man was pawing through

143

the drawer, under the counter, a frown on his face. Quist said, "What's wrong, lose something?"

Bancroft looked up. "There used to be a short-barrelled six-shooter under this money drawer—a thirty-two—here. Gave it to Grimes in case somebody tried to hold him up some night. I just noticed it wasn't here. Grimes likely doesn't even know it's gone. I know he's never shot it—"

"You sure?" Quist asked.

Bancroft's scowl deepened thoughtfully, then he shook his head. "Not our Nelly—"his lips twitched a little.

"The sheriff," Quist reminded, "was trying to find somebody around here to blame for shooting through Miss Bancroft's door."

Bancroft laughed suddenly. "It wouldn't be Grimes. He'd have no reason for an action like that. Actually, he's beholden to Helen—"

"For what?"

"She gave him a job, didn't she?"

Quist nodded. Bancroft ceased his search. The two men talked a few moments longer, then Quist headed for the hot sunlight of Main Street. Ten minutes later he was pouring cool beer into a glass at Heinz' Texas Bar. He was conversing idly with Heinz, when Jake Kiernan entered. Quist spoke to him but got nothing but a surly nod in reply. Kiernan asked for whisky. Heinz set out a bottle and glass. Kiernan poured a stiff drink, downed it and placed some money on the bar. His face looked angry, as though he were trying to hold his temper and not quite succeeding, when he turned to Quist.

"It's come out just as I said," he snapped.

Quist looked surprised, "What are you talking about, Sheriff —the chicken out of the egg?"

"And I don't want no smart-alecky answers, neither," Kiernan rasped. "I said if you stayed here, you'd make trouble." Quist looked questioning. The sheriff went on, "This Worden

144

trouble last night. Larrabee should have come after me—"

"Worden shoots at me and *I* make trouble?" Quist smiled.

"It wouldn't have happened, if you hadn't been here," Kiernan said wrathfully.

"I'm here on orders—" Quist commenced.

"And you're going to leave on orders," Kiernan cut in. "You're not wanted in Arcanum City. I'm going to see that you leave, if I have to go straight to the governor of this territory—"

Quist broke into sudden laughter. "The governor is going to start bucking the T.N. & A.S., Kiernan? Think again. My railroad helped to elect the governor. Go ahead, make your protest to him, but I warn you, you may get your sit-spot in a sling. You may anyway, even if you never approach the governor."

Kiernan cooled a trifle. He said cautiously, "What do you mean by that?"

Quist said curtly, "You come in here getting proddy with me, and you'll hear a few things you don't like. First, I could bring a charge of concealing evidence against you, Sheriff."

Kiernan wilted a little. He glanced nervously around and seemed relieved that he and Quist were the only customers. Paddy Heinz was at the far end of the bar, eyeing curiously the two men. "Wha—what do you mean, Quist?" Kiernan stammered.

"The night Vance Callister and his wife were murdered—"

"One was a suicide—" the sheriff started to point out.

"I'm telling you they were both murdered, and I don't give a damn who knows it. What kind of a sheriff are you to let anything of that sort go on under your nose—?"

"Y-Y-You're wrong, Quist. I'm asking for proof."

"You'll get it in good time, but for your information, somebody rode out to the ranch that night and killed those two—"

"I can't believe it. You're just crazy—"

"I'm asking where you were that night?"

"Hell's bells! I was here in town—until Stovepipe Hudson found me and—"

"Found you!" Quist snapped. "Maybe he was on your heels all the time. Stovepipe tells me he found you riding into town on a horse that looked like it had been run some. And you looked pretty hot and bothered yourself—"

"Oh, now, look here, Quist, that—" The sheriff choked a little and a sickly grin crossed his face. "You—you're not suspecting *me*—?"

"Why shouldn't I?" Quist snapped.

"I—I can explain everything." The sheriff was now anxious to please. "That night—sure I can explain it—I saw Alex Callister's horse running free along Mesquite Street. It slowed a minute and I tried to grab the reins. The gawddamn horse just jerked away, every time I got near. It swerved past me and started for Main Street. What could I do? I grabbed somebody's horse standing at a hitchrack, got in the saddle and took after the beast. It run clear out Main through those Mex shacks, and even then I had a hell of a time catching it with a rope that was on the saddle. Sure I looked hot and bothered. I was mad as hell—"

"I hope you can prove this."

"Hell! I can prove it by my deputy. When I brung back the damn' horse I saw Rod and I turned it over to him. Then I returned the horse I'd been forking to the hitchrail where I found it."

"A likely story," Quist scoffed.

"Now, look here, Quist," the sheriff started placatingly, "let's you and me have a drink and talk this over. All this talk of murder is nonsense, isn't it?"

"It's not nonsense. And I had a drink with you yesterday. Remember? I paid for it. Maybe you'll remember why, too. S'long, Kiernan. And let's have a better alibi the next time we meet."

Without giving the sheriff time to reply, Quist nodded to Paddy Heinz, turned and strode from the saloon. He was chuckling when he hit the sidewalk. "Maybe that will keep the fat fool off my tail for a spell," he mused.

Behind him the doors of the saloon banged apart, and the sheriff emerged, looking extremely worried, and headed diagonally across Main in the direction of his office. Quist swung about and re-entered the Texas Bar. "I think I can use another beer, Paddy."

Heinz set out the drink. "You sort of upset Jake, Mr. Quist."

Quist poured a glass of amber foaming fluid. "I intended to. He's too important for his own good."

"I figure you are right. Before you come here he heard about you and said if you set foot here he'd run you out. I don't know what's come over Jake. Used to be a fine feller. I guess maybe it was them women caused it. And he and Vance Callister was good friends once. But he fought with Vance and he's crabby with everybody—"

"What women you talking about, Paddy?"

"Miss Bancroft and her sister that married Callister."

"Where do they come in?"

"Like mebbe you've heard, Jake Kiernan is an old bach. But when Helen Bancroft come here, he began shinin' up to her. Hung around the hotel all the time. He used to come here regular, then he started spending his days and nights in the Arcanum House Bar. Next thing we knowed—the whole town was watching him—Vance Callister was top-dawg with Miss Helen. It looked like he'd marry her. So, Jake he starts sparkin' her sister, Anne. But Callister married Anne. And now Jake is back hanging around Helen every time he gets a chance. But he was sure sore at Vance Callister—"

"About what?"

"They were arguing in here one day. Jake claimed Callister was just cuttin' him out with the girls to be nasty. Callister sort of sneered at the sheriff. One thing led to another and hard words were passed. I heard Jake say he'd square accounts some day. Callister just laughed and told him he'd better go hang his tin star on somebody his own class. From then on the two never spoke to each other."

Quist looked thoughtful. "Interesting," he said half to himself. "No wonder Kiernan didn't like him."

"Look, Mr. Quist, is it true what you said about murder—?"

"That's the way it looks to me, Paddy."

"Wait till news of that gets out—or maybe I should keep my trap shut?"

Quist shrugged his shoulders. "I know of no reason for keeping it closed."

Five minutes later when he left the saloon he mused, "And now the news will be all over town. Which is what I want. It may pull the murderer into the open that much sooner, if he thinks he has to try something drastic. I just want a little more proof, just a little more. It was tried last night. They may be even more careless next time." He chuckled suddenly. "I wasn't too careful myself."

He sauntered on, walking east, giving answering nods to one or two men who spoke to him. Everett Bancroft and Nelly Grimes stood talking in front of the doorway of the Arcanum House lobby. Bancroft's face was like a thundercloud; Grimes looked frightened. Quist couldn't hear what they were saying, but Grimes kept shaking his head, as though he were denying or protesting something. Bancroft looked up, saw Quist approaching. He said something more to Grimes and Grimes headed for the lobby, looking like a frightened rabbit. Bancroft gave a short wave of one hand to Quist and also withdrew to the interior of the hotel.

"Now, I wonder what that was all about," Quist speculated. "Maybe I should go in and—" He broke off, noticing Dodge Randall lounging against the tie-rail in front of Ziebold's Livery Stable, and, deciding it was time to talk to Randall, crossed Main diagonally from the hotel corner. Randle saw him when he stepped to the plank sidewalk, lifted one hand in a greeting, "Hi-yuh, Mr. Quist."

"How's it going, Dodge? Where's your slip-horn?"

Randall shoved his sombrero farther to the back of his head. "I sure wish I had it with me, Mr. Quist. T'tell the truth I had to take it to my uncle. I left it with him for safekeeping. Just so's I wouldn't get lonesome, he let me have some money to carry. Trouble is, I got hungry one night and spent the money."

"Too bad." Quist took a position beside Randall, propped against the tie-rail, facing the building across the sidewalk. Quist produced Durham and papers, rolled a cigarette and passed the "makin's" to Randall. A match was scratched. Smoke drifted in the air, vanished. Quist said, "You had some money last night, though."

"Yeah?" Surprise in Randall's tones. "What gives you that idea—hey, wait a minute, I'll bet you saw me giving Hunk Worden—" He paused, "Quite a tanglement you had with Hunk last night. Do you suppose he's up there with the angels playing a harp?"

"Probably a slip-horn," Quist stated, straight-faced. "You were saying something about money, Dodge."

"Sure, I was returning some money—hundred bucks it was—that Worden let me have—"

Quist laughed caustically. "From what I hear, Hunk Worden never had that much money before in his life—"

Randall grinned. "Hell, I don't mean Worden had loaned it to me. You see, we been having a little poker game, every night, in one of the back stalls in the stable. Poor Hunk, his cards always run the wrong way. Me, I do all right. Lucky, maybe. So Hunk he gives me this hundred and asks me to play it for him, and I was to get a percentage—"

Quist yawned widely. Randall said, "Don't you believe it? We play every night. You can ask Ziebold. He lets us have a stall—"

"I'm not questioning that part."

"What's bothering you, Mr. Quist?"

"The thought that you'd give him money."

"Gawd's truth. Hunk was thinking he was bad luck. He didn't even come to the game last night. I felt sort of bad. Actually, I got to thinking my luck would change and I'd lose poor Hunk's money. So I just never played it a-tall. Later I give it back to him. You must have seen me and jumped to conclusions—"

"I'll jump on your back in a minute."

"Aw-w, now, Mr. Quist, don't you be that way. You could make it difficult for me." His jaw dropped suddenly. "My Gawd, I'll bet you got to thinking I'd paid Worden to take a shot at you."

Quist laughed softly. "Why, Dodge, it just never entered my mind."

"Naturally not," Randall said quickly. "What am I thinking of? You'd know I'd never have any money, even if I had the idea, which same I wouldn't. I got no reason to harm you."

"And that's your story," Quist said. "You could do yourself a lot of good, Dodge, if you'd talk a mite."

"About what? I know nothing. T'tell the truth I just got to wondering where Hunk got that money. Say, that's a sort of mystery. He was such a big dumb lunkhead, in a way. 'Course" —piously—"I shouldn't talk about the dead that way—"

"Let's forget it." Quist sighed. "What do you hear from Ed Jamison, these days, Dodge?"

"Who?" Randall frowned. "Who is Ed—?"

"Don't overdo it, Dodge," Quist cautioned softly.

Sudden comprehension flooded Randall's swarthy features. "Oh, sure, Mr. Quist, sure—you mean my old roommate in the school for wayward boys, up Utah way. Damned if I could think who you was talking about for a minute. Say, Mr. Quist, you have

150

been checking up on me, haven't you? Well, it's to be expected, I suppose. I got a rep. You have to play safe. No hard feelings, y'understand. Cripes! I haven't give a thought to Ed since I left. I suppose he's still in the same grade, toiling over his studies, regretting he ever let his trigger-finger slip that way. But he'll take his lesson to heart, just like I did. He'll come out a better fellow—"

"He's already out," Quist cut in. He exhaled a cloud of cigarette smoke, dropped the butt on the sidewalk and put his toe on it.

"You don't say." Randall looked surprised. "I thought he'd have to stay a while and make up back studies. How is the old professor these days—"

"The *warden*," Quist said, "sounded riled in the telegram I got from him yesterday. Seems Jamison was paroled a couple of months back on condition he take a job in Salt Lake City. He took the job all right, and then something over a month back he failed to show up and report. He just plain vanished. The authorities have a hunch he headed for Canada—"

"Broke parole, eh?" Randall said indignantly. Suddenly he snickered. "Now that's a downright dirty trick to play on the old professor. It'll go hard with Ed when they catch him. Canada? Don't you believe it, Mr. Quist. I remember Ed said once he didn't like cold climates. I'll be damned. I'll bet if they catch him, they'll keep him after school—"

"Chop it off," Quist cut in savagely. "If you know where Jamison is it would be good policy to tell me—"

"Aw, now, Mr. Quist," Randall said reprovingly, "no need for you to get riled at me. I'd do anything I could to keep friends with you, but if I don't know where Ed went, you can't expect me—anyway"—taking a new tack—"what do you care about Ed? He never did nothing to your choo-choo line. Ain't you got enough to keep you busy, right here?"

151

Quist grinned suddenly, feeling the man was laughing inwardly at him. He drew a dollar bill from his pocket and stuffed it into one pocket of Randall's flimsy vest. "I'll see you again, Dodge," he said, starting to leave.

Randall caught at his sleeve. "Hey, what's this buck for?"

"You've been singing such a nice tune I thought maybe you could buy another slip-horn. You've been making just the kind of music I like to hear."

Quist glanced back at the man once as he headed along the sidewalk. Randall was standing, bill in hand, staring, frowning, after him. Quist chuckled, "I've got him wondering now, if he really did spill something he shouldn't have."

Quist sauntered on as far as Concho Street, crossed the street and started back. Just before he reached the 1st National Bank of Arcanum City, he encountered Rod Larrabee. The two men stopped to talk a minute. The deputy said, "News spreads fast, Greg. It's all over town already that you claim there was a double murder at the Box-VC. Did you want it that way?" Quist nodded. Larrabee went on, "You must have put some sort of firecracker under Doc Iverson last night, too."

"Where'd you get that idea?"

"He was in town about an hour ago. Looks like he'd been sick—"

"He has been."

"Steady on his pins, though. He's rented that vacant store next door to the saddle shop. Told me he was going to open an office and see if he couldn't take some of the load off Forbes' shoulders."

"Good for Luke. He's a smart doctor, Rod. I think he'll make it all right. All he needed was just somebody to show faith in him."

Larrabee nodded. "Maybe I haven't done all I could—"

"You sure haven't. Rod, you never told me that the night the

152

Callisters were killed, Alex's pony was found running free on the streets."

The small man crimsoned. "Where'd you hear that?"

"From Jake Kiernan. He claims to have caught the pony and turned it over to you. That correct?"

Larrabee avoided Quist's eyes. He said finally, "Yes—I reckon. Leastwise, I saw Jake leading the pony in from the west end of town. He told me to take care of it. I recognized the pony and took it over to the stage stables. Tied it there. I didn't know where Alex was—"

"Why didn't you tell me this before?" Quist snapped. The deputy didn't reply. Quist went on, "I'll tell you why. You feared Alex was mixed up in that business, somehow. Even if you weren't on speaking terms with her, you were trying to cover up for her. You were afraid she'd been out there—"

"You're right, Greg." The small man faced Quist squarely, but his voice was miserable. "I'm sorry as the devil."

"All right, forget it," Quist said gruffly. "Let's go get a beer before dinner. Walking in the sun makes me thirsty." He added, "If I'm to get anyplace, I've got to have your full cooperation."

"You'll get it"—fervently. "I'm just thinking, Greg. Do you suppose Jake spoke the truth. I'd not seen him for a spell that night."

"I don't know whether Kiernan was speaking truth or not," Quist stated grumpily. "Something else you never told me—that Kiernan and Callister were on bad terms."

Larrabee shrugged. "I never felt that meant much. Jake's pride was hurt when Callister cut him out—first with Helen and then Anne—say, where'd you hear this?"

"Paddy Heinz. The two men had words there one day. Kiernan accused Callister of being nasty or hoggish or something. He stated he'd get even some day."

"Lord, I never knew that. Still, I don't think Jake would carry

153

out a threat of that sort. At bottom, he's a pretty good hombre."

"At bottom, maybe," Quist growled. "But you don't know what he might have done if he blowed his top."

XVII

THE INQUEST that afternoon completely absolved Quist of all blame in the matter of Hunk Worden's death. No one came forward to claim the body; he was not known to have any relatives. At the sheriff's suggestion, the hundred dollars found in the dead man's pocket, was to be spent for burial purposes and a stone to be erected over his grave in the town Boot Hill which lay on the south side of the T.N. & A.S. railroad tracks.

With the inquest out of the way, Quist paid a visit to Holt Traxler, president of the bank. Traxler was a portly, bald-headed man with cold eyes and a rat-trap mouth. Quist didn't take to him, but he had to admit Traxler greeted him genially enough when he invited him to a seat in his office. The man produced a box of cigars from his desk and passed them across to Quist. They lighted up and Traxler asked, "What can I do for you, Mr. Quist?"

"I'd like to ask one or two questions. If they conflict with the best interests of your bank, just tell me so. First, where do you stand in regard to Alex Callister and the Bancrofts? In short, whose side are you on?"

Traxler said heavily, "I think the fact the bank attorney-at-law is handling Alexandra Callister's interests, should answer that question. When the case comes to court, this fall—"

"I'm asking you personally. I understand Callister had a heavy interest in this bank, so it's natural the bank would—"

"Not necessarily," Traxler snapped. "But if it's my personal opinion you want, I'm all on Alexandra's side. She's a fine girl;

I've known her since she was born. Regardless what the will says, or how the court decides—particularly in view of this rumor I hear that you claim both Vance and his wife were murdered—"

"I hope to be able to prove that," Quist said quietly.

"—I feel Alexandra is entitled to her father's money."

"What have you got against the Bancrofts?"

"Nothing. I scarcely know Everett Bancroft. I find Helen Bancroft a very pleasant woman." A smile twitched at his thin lips; the banker exterior cracked a little. He gazed from his window, then his eyes came back to Quist. "In fact"—something wistful in his tones—"she's considerable woman, the sort that makes a man wish he were younger."

"I know exactly what you mean," Quist chuckled.

The banker pursed his lips and frowned, as though he'd let down the bars too far. "Anyway, you'll understand why Vance fell so hard for her. Personally I thought him foolish, at his age, but Vance wasn't the man to listen to reason, even if I'd told him so—which I didn't even think of doing."

"However, he didn't marry Helen. Why?"

Traxler shrugged thick shoulders, dropped cigar ash in a metal tray. "I haven't the least idea. Vance never told *me,* at least. Maybe he just decided he liked Anne Bancroft better. Have you heard of any reason?"

"Nothing I care to repeat at the moment. When did you first meet Helen Bancroft?"

"When she came here to make a deal for the hotel. We had the handling of the Arcanum House. We'd advertised it for sale, as we wanted to close an estate. Miss Bancroft came here, told us of her experience. She had just sold a small hotel in Baton Rouge. She seemed capable. We were favorably impressed, except on one point—"

"What was that?"

"She had not enough money to swing the deal, and wanted the

bank to loan her the money. Our board of directors considered the matter and turned her down. There was one dissenting vote —Vance Callister's. He was all for giving her backing. After all, he was one of the founders of the bank—a heavy stockholder. His word carried weight. He tried to ride roughshod over the rest of us. That caused hard feelings, too. The upshot of the matter was that Vance said if the bank wouldn't lend her the money, he would. We compromised. The bank loaned some backing; Callister loaned the bulk of the money. And refused interest on his loan. Oh, he was hard hit from the start. We could all see that."

"Why were the directors against the loan?"

"We'd heard Miss Bancroft's plans. The hotel was old and needed repairs. If she'd been satisfied with that—well, she wasn't. She planned to put draperies at the windows, carpeting on all the floors, new furniture where necessary. All of which she did, of course, when the loan went through."

Quist frowned. "I've seen lots worse hotels. What was wrong with her ideas?"

"Too much fixing up before this town is large enough to support a hotel like that. Actually, there aren't enough rooms to warrant such expenditure. The rates had to be raised, of course. That sent many people to the Miners' & Cattlemen's Hotel, up on Concho and Main. I've heard the place called a fleabag, but at least the owner doesn't owe the bank money."

"How has Miss Bancroft been on payments?"

"She's fallen behind. The interest is mounting. Actually, unless the court decides in her favor, I'm afraid the bank will be forced to foreclose. She knows how to run a hotel all right, but this time she just bit off more than she could chew. She's no doubt discovered that this is far different from operating a small inn in Baton Rouge."

There was a thoughtful glint in Quist's topaz eyes when he left the bank. He chewed savagely on his cigar, then distastefully,

156

tossed it to the road. "There's sure some greedy people in the world," he grunted savagely.

That night after supper, Quist emerged from the hotel dining room and stopped a moment in the lobby to talk to Nelly Grimes who was looking extremely worried. There was no one else in the lobby at the time. Grimes gave Quist a sort of startled nod, when he looked up from his desk. Quist said, "You look sort of upset, Mr. Grimes. Anything wrong?"

"No—well—er—no nothing, Mr. Quist. Just one of my bad days I guess. Mr. Bancroft has been rather disagreeable—"

"About what?"

Grimes was evasive. "Oh, just the running of this desk, I guess. I'm supposed to be on nights only, but he's always insisting I help out during the day. I never get my proper rest. I wish he'd never come here. Miss Helen was never so bossy. He has the awfullest temper—flies off the handle at the least thing. Always suspecting things that aren't so. As if I'd ever do a thing like that—"

"Like what?"

Grimes' mouth closed primly. "I wouldn't think of discussing management affairs with a guest, Mr. Quist."

"You're right, of course. With Bancroft so hot-tempered, I'll bet he hit the ceiling the night Vance Callister and Anne died."

"He was real upset all right. He and Helen had talked all evening of driving out that night and visiting—Everett had just arrived the day before and hadn't seen Anne in years—but Helen was too busy here to get away. Then, when the news came, he just acted sort of stunned as though he couldn't believe it. On top of that he had his hands full with Miss Helen. My! She was almost prostrated. Next she was all for going out to the ranch, at once, but Everett finally persuaded her to stay here. He had to assist her to her room, and I was sent to buy smelling salts. It was all terrible—" Grimes broke off.

A tall, bulky-shouldered man, wearing a sheriff's star-of-office

157

on his lapel had entered the lobby, carrying a small satchel. He registered and received a room-key. Quist heard Grimes call him Sheriff Burks. Some comment was made regarding the sheriff's arriving by stagecoach from Black Ore Springs a few minutes previously. Then, Quist heard the sheriff inquiring where he could find Gregory Quist. Quist turned toward the desk.

"I'm Quist," he said. Grimes performed an introduction.

"I came all the way here to see you, Mr. Quist, and give you some information regarding that trouble on the stage route, two days ago." Ott Burks was deeply tanned, with a wide brown mustache and shrewd eyes. His broad-brimmed Stetson and clothing were dusty.

"Do you want to save it until later?" Quist asked. "The dining room will close soon. You'll just have time to wash up and get supper. I'll go up with you and show you where my room is."

They ascended the stairway. Burks' room was across from Quist's. Quist entered his own room, opened a bottle of bourbon, turned the lamp higher and sat down to wait.

Half an hour later, Quist was listening to the sheriff from Acacia County. "Larrabee sent me word of what had happened to you and Miss Callister, just this side of Wood's Diggings. He informed me you were busy here. We'd already suspected some skulduggery before we heard from Larrabee. One, of Black Ore Springs' no-good characters named Dike Arden visited our local doctor that afternoon, with a wound in his neck. Claimed he'd had an accident while hunting."

Quist poured a neat three-fingers of bourbon for the sheriff and opened a bottle of beer. Burks continued, "Dike Arden had a buckshot lodged in his neck. He refused to say who had shot him. The doctor got suspicious and threw a scare into him. Arden was bleeding like a stuck pig and the doc told him the shot had hit the jugular vein and Arden couldn't last long. Arden broke down and implicated a man named Charley Biggs. Said Biggs shot him by accident."

"Biggs worked as shotgun guard for the stage line, but quit that day at Black Ore Springs."

"So we learned from Buzzard Greer. Buzzard suggested we look for another Arden pal, named Yoakum. I arrested Biggs, but he just wouldn't give any plausible account of the wound in Arden's neck, and said Arden had shot himself by accident. The two of 'em argued about that, so I threw 'em both in the cooler, until I could learn more. Arden wa'n't hurt bad. Just scared for a spell. Then he turned sullen and wouldn't talk. That night, a station man from Honey-Pod Ranch—name of Tom—arrived and told us what had happened."

Burks paused for a swallow of whisky and went on, "Then the following day, I got word from Larrabee giving some details. By that time, me and my deputy had gone out and got Yoakum's body. We brought it in, got it packed in ice now, waiting for the inquest."

"And you want me to return with you for the inquest?"

" 'Twon't be necessary. You just tell me what happened, I'll write out a statement and you sign it. I understand you got your hands full here." Quist talked a few minutes and Burks resumed, "My deputy ain't no fool and he hates law-busters worse'n poison. Sometimes he's inclined to get a mite rough with a stubborn prisoner that won't talk. But he was determined to get at the bottom of the business and he worked Arden and Biggs over in separate cells, until they finally moaned out stories that agreed. You understand—"apologetically—"sometimes we got to get a mite harsh with crooks."

"What was the story?"

"Yoakum, Biggs and Arden were to be paid one hundred each —fifty down and fifty when the job was done—to hold up the stage and kidnap Alexandra Callister. She was to be kept captive up in the hills until—well, none of them three scuts knew what she was to be held for, I guess; that was to be decided later. Biggs admitted that maybe she'd eventually be killed if things didn't go right. We're holding them for trial, of course—"

"I don't suppose you know who paid them the money?"

"Yeah, we worked that out of 'em too. They was glad to tell, to save their own skins as much as possible. The feller that promoted the job had been in Black Ore Springs a few days before and made the deal with 'em. His name was Randall—Dodge Randall. What's up, you recognize the name?"

"I recognize it," Quist said grimly.

"Must be somebody local, then. I know I had 'quiries made around Black Ore Springs. They never heard of him there."

"I know where to get him," Quist said tersely, "but maybe I'll have to move fast. You want to come?"

"I'll leave it to you. I've had a long trip and I'm a mite weary. While you're gone, I'll write out a statement for you to sign."

They moved from the room. Quist nodded shortly and left the sheriff to enter his own room, then hurried down the stairway. He only half noticed that Everett Bancroft was still heckling Nelly Grimes at the desk in the lobby as he passed, and almost collided with Rod Larrabee at the entrance to the hotel.

Before Larrabee could start speaking, Quist snapped, "I want Dodge Randall. Fast! Pick him up, Rod, if you see him first. You head east from here and I'll go west. Hurry now!"

The deputy nodded and darted away, scanning both sides of the street. Quist paused a moment. There were quite a few people on the streets, horses and vehicles were lined at hitchracks here and there. Lights from buildings threw broad splashes of yellow across the sidewalks and road. Quist had just started to cross Mesquite Street when he saw Dodge Randall heading toward Ziebold's Livery on the opposite corner. Quist raised his voice and hailed the man.

Reluctantly, Randall stopped in the middle of the road.

"Want to talk to you a minute, Dodge," Quist said, as he approached.

"Sure, Mr. Quist," Randall said, only a few paces separating the men now, "but how about making it fast? I don't want to be late for our poker game."

"You can forget the poker game, Dodge. Figure on talking instead. Dike Arden and Charley Biggs have talked. I think it's your turn now."

"Aw, Mr. Quist, I don't know what you're talking about . . ."

Even while the man was speaking, his right hand darted to the holster at his right thigh.

Quist's hand flashed beneath his coat, the short-barreled forty-four swept into view, spouting lead and flame even before Quist found his mark, bullets spitting up dust at Randall's feet and ranging higher. The heavy detonations echoed along the street.

Randall's single shot flew wild overhead as he sagged back, swept from his feet by the impact of Quist's heavy slugs. The gun flew from his hand to the roadway, as he struck the earth on his left shoulder, then folded to an awkward sprawl, one leg straight out, the other bent at the knee. Burned powder smoke drifted in the air.

Wild yells sounded along the street. Those who had ducked for shelter at the first report now emerged cautiously and began to form a crowd about the wounded man. Quist snapped at the first man, "Go get Doc Iverson. Move, dammit!" He requested someone else to get a glass of whisky, then stooped at Randall's side, pillowing Randall's head on the man's sombrero. Randall was ashen white, his eyes closed. Blood welled on the right side of his shirt. A flask of whisky was thrust into Quist's hand. Quist removed the cork and placed the mouth of the flask to Randall's lips.

Randall choked, coughed, then swallowed some of the fiery liquor. After a few moments his pale-blue eyes opened and he gazed vacantly around. Then they cleared, focusing on Quist's face. Something like a laugh parted his lips, as he murmured,

161

"Seems like you're—always teaching me—to live different—Mr. Quist. I should've knowed better—than—to draw against—you—"

"Maybe you'd best do some talking now," Quist urged.

"Sure—anything you want—to know—"

Quist heard Rod Larrabee's breathless voice at his shoulder, but didn't answer at once. He was giving Randall another drink of bourbon.

Then Doctor Iverson's voice, commanding, irritable: "Goddamn it!" Iverson swore. "Haven't you folks got sense enough to move back and give him air? Go on, scat, the whole of you!" The crowd moved back, Larrabee with them. Quist rose and faced the doctor. He said low-voiced, "I don't think it's too bad. I tried to—"

"Better let me decide that," Iverson snapped. He put down his bag, opened it, knelt at Randall's side. Somebody pushed through the crowd carrying an oil lamp, the flame wavering, smoking the chimney, and set it near the kneeling doctor. Larrabee ordered the crowd to the sidewalk. Quist stood well back with the crowd, waiting for Iverson's decision, shoving fresh loads in his six-shooter.

It came after a minute. Iverson rose, walked toward Quist, leaving the prone man flat in the center of the road. No one stood near him now. Iverson said to Quist, "Nothing to worry about. And I won't go technical on you. Right arm broken, right collar bone ditto. Get him down to my office and I'll probe out those slugs—"

Abruptly, Quist saw Randall's body jerk convulsively, even before his ears caught the detonation of the gun. There came a panicky rush of the men along the sidewalk, as they scattered wildly. Randall lay very still now. Quist swore, eyes darting along the street, trying to determine from which direction the shot had come. Larrabee ranged through the crowd arbitrarily jerking guns from holsters and feeling their barrels. Quist joined him, both asking questions, but were met with only negative replies. No one, it appeared, knew where the shot had originated.

Iverson was back at Randall's body again. He rose after a couple of minutes, shaking his head. "Don't bother taking him to my office. The undertaker's is nearer."

XVIII

IT WAS near midnight when Quist returned to his room. He mounted the steps wearily, having disregarded Nelly Grimes' horrified comments on the shooting. He was scarcely in his room when a knock sounded. He opened it to admit Sheriff Burks. Burks had the statement ready for him to sign. The sheriff said, "Randall's dead, eh?"

Quist nodded and swore. "I did my damnedest not to hit him fatally, and then—" He broke off, drawing a long sigh of frustration.

"I was out. Several people told me what had happened. No idea where that last shot came from, eh?"

"Somebody's upper window is the best we can guess at it. Doc Iverson did an autopsy. The bullet entered at a sharp angle, that's all we can say. Blast the luck! Randall would have been ready to talk shortly. Oh, yes, Rod Larrabee said to say hello to you. He won't have time to get around. He's making some sort of canvass of the town, checking people and upper-story windows. Sheriff Kiernan is fit to be tied. He was at his boarding-house when it happened. Says I've made more trouble—"

"I don't see how the sheriff can blame you, but then Jake never was long on reasoning. Well, if I'm going to catch that seven-o'clock stage home, I'd better get to bed."

Quist thanked him for coming to Arcanum City and the sheriff departed for his room. Quist undressed and went to bed, thinking, That slug could have been meant for me, but I doubt it. Randall was in plain view. I was back with the crowd. Iverson had just started toward me. That oil lamp still stood near Randall . . .

Two hours later, unable to sleep, Quist rose and drew on his trousers. He knew the angle at which the fatal bullet had entered Randall's body, but exactly how had Randall been lying at the time? In order to better visualize the scene once more, Quist left his room, walking silently on bare feet, and made his way out to the upper gallery. He noticed as he stepped out that the section of railing where Worden's body had gone through, had been repaired. The gallery lay in the shadow of its roof, though a bright moon floated overhead, throwing objects along the silent street into bold relief. Quist moved down to the far, west end of the gallery and stood gazing beyond the railing. A dim light burned in a window of Ziebold's Livery. It was only a few paces from the livery that Randall had died.

The night breeze carried a chill. The gallery flooring was cold under Quist's bare feet. He swore inwardly: even seeing the street once more didn't seem to help. He fought back the feeling of discouragement that rose in his breast and started back for his room. One foot struck something on the floor, something that rolled with a tiny, metallic sound before it stopped. Stooping, Quist groped about in the gloom. When he found the object, he knew by the feel what it was. A moment later, he was back in his room, lighting his lamp. The object he had found proved to be an exploded forty-four shell. "Somebody," Quist mused, "had best be a mite more careful about where they eject their shells. Maybe this is the break I need."

This time when his head struck the pillow, he went promptly to sleep.

The following morning when he entered the dining room for breakfast, he found Helen Bancroft standing near a table at which sat Urban Jarrell, the "boy lawyer," as Quist had begun to think of him. Helen turned to him and nodded a bright "good morning," and started to show him to a table. "I'll sit with Mr. Jarrell, if he has no objection," Quist said. Whether the man had any objections or not, Quist gave him no time to voice them as he dropped into a seat across the table from the would-be lawyer. Helen beckoned the Mexican waitress to come take Quist's order, then lingered a minute longer, saying:

"You know, Mr. Quist, I think Mr. Jarrell is more concerned than I am about that shot that entered my door a couple of nights back. He seems to feel I'm in momentary danger of losing my life."

Quist laughed softly, eyeing with undisguised admiration Helen's very blond hair and dark eyes. This morning she wore modest gray; there was a pencil stuck in her shining wealth of corn-silk hair. She looked completely the very successful operator of a first-class hotel, but there was something more as well. Quist glanced at Jarrell and judged that the young fellow was more in danger of losing his heart than Helen Bancroft her life. He was red-faced, stammering.

"It's true," he insisted, doggedly. "There's no telling what may happen before the fall court sits. The sooner the business is settled, the better for everyone. It's not safe."

"Then you really feel, Mr. Jarrell," Helen said, "that I should ask my lawyer to try to get the date of the case set ahead."

"Definitely," Jarrell stated. "In your place I'd write this morning."

"What do you think, Mr. Quist?"

"I learned a long time back, Miss Helen, not to argue with lawyers. They have a habit of putting things in your mouth you never intended to say, if you let 'em get away with it."

"To tell the truth," Helen said, "I'm not so concerned about danger to my life, as I am about the way that poor man was shot down last night—pardon me, Mr. Quist, perhaps you don't care to talk about it—but Arcanum City could get a bad name."

Quist nodded without saying anything. The waitress came with Quist's ham and eggs, and Helen drifted out of the dining room after pausing a moment with one or two other diners to pass conversation. Quist glanced at Jarrell who was staring sulkily at him. "Better finish your breakfast, sonny," Quist suggested. "There's a long time until dinner."

"I've eaten all I care for"—sullenly.

Quist lifted the coffee cup to his lips. "Something seems to be eating you, then. What's wrong?"

"You just won't listen to sense," Jarrell burst out. "Miss Bancroft's life has already been endangered. I demand that you write to our home office and suggest it petition for a special sitting of court. Then this business could be settled and we could go ahead with the purchase of the right-of-way—"

"You demand?" Quist asked coldly.

Jarrell's eyes slid sidewise. "Well, you know what I mean. But common sense should tell you I've done all I can." Once started, the words flowed from his mouth in an angry stream. "Here, somebody shoots through Miss Bancroft's door. Undoubtedly an attempt to murder her. You're just stubborn, Quist. Here I take all the risk—"

"What risk?" Quist snapped, comprehension beginning to dawn.

Jarrell reddened, bit his lip. "Well, I don't mean risk, exactly," he commenced lamely. "It's just that I've given a lot of thought to this case and it seems to me—well, I could have been studying in Mr. Nordwall's office instead of wasting my days . . ."

His voice drifted to silence. Quist looked steadily at him a moment, then went on eating. Jarrell shifted uneasily in his chair. Once he started to leave. Quist told him to sit down and he reseated himself without protest. Something of fright showed in his face now. When Quist had had another cup of coffee and put money on the table, he said to Jarrell, "Come on, bud." Jarrell asked where they were going. Quist said, "To your room. I want to talk to you."

In silence they ascended the stairway from the lobby, Jarrell hanging back like a whipped puppy. In the upper hallway he produced his key and with trembling hand unlocked the door. He looked very white now. Quist entered; reluctantly Jarrell followed and closed the door. Quist looked around and saw a room furnished much like his own, though smaller. There were some papers on a table and a copy of *Blackstone's Commentaries*. Quist turned, fastened Jarrell with a long hard look and snapped, "Where's the gun?"

"Wha—what gun—Mr. Quist?"

"You know damned well what gun," Quist said harshly. "If I have to search it out myself it will be the worse for you."

Jarrell's shoulders slumped. He went to the dresser, drew out a drawer and fumbled at the bottom of a pile of shirts and underwear, then handed the weapon to Quist. It was a thirty-two caliber, with barrel less then three inches long, the same model, in fact, that Larrabee had removed from Nelly Grimes' cash drawer.

"Where in God's name did you get this?" Quist demanded.

Jarrell swallowed hard. "Everybody told me when I came out to Texas I should always carry a gun. So—so I bought one."

"You simple, unmitigated fool," Quist said angrily. He slipped the gun into his pocket. "Do you know you could be sent to prison for what you did. I have only to pass the word to Miss Bancroft and if she laid a complaint—"

"I didn't mean her any harm," Jarrell whined. "I shot low so it wouldn't hit her—"

"And then jumped back into your room and closed the door. You miserable idiot! And then you thought I'd ask Jay Fletcher to get a special early session of court to settle things. And the right-of-way would be put through, sooner than contemplated. Figured to scare hell out of Helen Bancroft and get her to appeal to her lawyer on the grounds her life was endangered. By God, I should turn you up and gun-whip you—but not with this pea-shooter."

"I—I didn't mean any real harm. I was just trying to help our company—"

"To hell with that, Jarrell. And if you could have put it across, then you'd gone back and boasted what you'd done. You were going to be the bright genius of the law, weren't you, the boy prodigy. Munson Nordwall would then promote you over the heads of all the other legal clerks. Hell's bells on a tomcat! As if I didn't have enough other problems here, without you mess-ing things up."

"Wha—what are you going to do, Mr. Quist?"

"What I'm going to do is none of your damned business. What you're going to do is pack your bag and head back to El Paso on the first eastbound you can catch. You've only got about fifteen minutes before that train comes through. If you miss that train, so help me God, I'll have the sheriff throw you in a cell. Get busy, now. And tell Munson J. Nordwall if he messes up my trail with any more half-baked, wet-behind-the-ears law sharps, I'll see personally that his contract with the company is can-celed."

Quist strode from the room and slammed the door. He paused a moment, listening. From Jarrell's room came a frantic slam-ming of dresser drawers and the sounds of clothing being crammed into a bag. Scowling angrily, Quist descended the stairs, stopped long enough in the lobby to tell Everett Bancroft to make up Jarrell's bill, then pushed on to the street.

Bancroft looked after him, frowning. "I'd suspect Mr. Quist of being in a bad temper this morning. Now I wonder what caused Jarrell's unexpected departure?" But when Jarrell paid his bill, Bancroft could extract no information from him, beyond the fact he'd been recalled to the home office in Texas.

Quist strode down Main, absent-mindedly touching his fingers

168

to sombrero brim when a woman with a parasol passed him, nodding curtly to two men who gave him pleasant greetings. At the sheriff's office he found Rod Larrabee, looking dejected. Larrabee said, "I've wracked my brains but I can't figure where that shot came from that killed Randall, last night. I've been around checking upper windows, and asking questions. Can't find anyone even suspicious—"

"Let it drop for a spell, Rod. Maybe I've found the shell, anyway."

He produced the exploded forty-four shell he'd found on the gallery the previous night. Larrabee's eyes widened. "Where did you get it?"

Quist told him. "Keep it under your hat, Rod. Anyway, this may not have been the ca'tridge that killed Dodge Randall."

"I'd bet it is. You were lucky in finding it."

"Somebody did me a favor by dropping it. I was lucky to pick it up. What? No, don't get me wrong, Rod. I never claimed that somebody living at the hotel fired this ca'tridge. Hell, it's not hard to reach that gallery. That upper hallway is generally deserted, unless a guest is coming or going. Nelly Grimes never pays any attention to who passes through the lobby or in and out of the bar. For that matter, we both know the gallery can be reached from the roof of the building next door. Hasn't the sheriff shown up yet?"

The small man shook his head. "Jake generally comes in around noon. Randall's killing last night kept him up late, so I imagine he'll sleep in at his boardinghouse."

Quist asked, "You still got Vance Callister's six-shooter in the safe?" Larrabee asked if he wanted to see it. Quist said he did. The deputy opened the safe and produced the weapon. Quist examined the spent shells in the cylinder, compared them to the shell he'd found on the gallery. Finally he returned the gun to Larrabee with the advice, "Hang on to that gun. No chance of anybody lifting it, is there?"

169

Larrabee frowned. "I don't see how there could be. Jake and I are the only ones who have the combination of the safe. I wouldn't remove it without a good reason, and I don't see why Jake should."

"I guess you're right, Rod," Quist nodded. "This empty shell wasn't fired from Callister's gun, that's certain. Oh, yes, here's something else to keep quiet about until I give the word. You don't need to bother any more about who threw that thirty-two slug into Helen Bancroft's door. I've got the gun."

"T'hell you say. And it wasn't Nelly Grimes' thirty-two?"

Quist shook his head. "I'm hanging on to Grimes' gun for the present, though." He took Jarrell's small revolver from his pocket and handed it to Larrabee. "Belonged to that boy lawyer who was staying at the hotel. He's already left. I ordered him to leave."

Larrabee was examining the gun. "*Hmm* . . . one cartridge exploded—five left. Same model as Nelly Grimes—" He paused, "How come Jarrell to take a shot at that door? Accident?"

"With malice aforethought you might say," Quist growled. "That gawddamned half-baked, chicken-livered—would you believe it, Jarrell, the simple fool, was going to get things settled in a hurry? He figured . . ." Quist went on and related what had happened.

The deputy heard him through in silence, then began to laugh. "Lord, that's one on you, Greg! On me and the sheriff too, I reckon."

"It's not funny," Quist growled. "Just keep it quiet for a time though. Jake Kiernan hates the T.N. & A.S. enough as it is. Damn! Seems like our legal department is always mixing things up for me." The humor of the situation appeared to him after a time and he conceded that the drinks were on him as he and Larrabee made their way across to the Texas Bar.

That afternoon Doctor Forbes as coroner—and with Doctor Iverson's assistance—held an inquest over the body of Dodge

170

Randall. Witnesses had been found who could swear they'd seen Randall pull his gun before Quist drew, so Quist was exonerated on that score, much to Jake Kiernan's disappointment; he had wanted Quist held for trial, or at least a further examination. Some attempt was made to discover what had caused the trouble between Quist and Randall, and with adroit statements Quist allowed the coroner's jury to believe that Randall had held a grudge because Quist had been instrumental in placing him behind bars previously.

As to the killer who had fired the fatal bullet into Dodge Randall's body, no light was forthcoming. The jury's verdict concluded: ". . . and the said Dodge Randall's death was due to a bullet wound fired by some person unknown." In addition, Sheriff Jake Kiernan was directed to take all necessary steps to at once find, apprehend and arrest said unknown.

XIX

A WEEK of impatient waiting ensued, with Quist almost ready to chew his fingernails down to the knuckles. He became testy, irritable, at not receiving the report for which he waited. He'd had but one cryptic telegram from Jay Fletcher stating that matters were being taken care of. Time dragged heavily on his hands. Each train as it drew in from the East found Quist on hand to greet its conductor, and the conductor's negative shake of the head produced considerable profanity from the impatient Quist.

He had gone riding once with Alexandra Callister. On another occasion he had bought supper for Alex and Rod Larrabee and with some envy had watched them leave, later, starry-eyed. In desperation he had even played checkers with Nelly Grimes one afternoon and had been soundly trounced, partly because his mind was on other things. However, he was beginning to believe that Grimes might be smarter than he had at first thought. At any rate, Grimes became more at ease; from time to time he hinted at certain troubles with Everett Bancroft, though what they were, Grimes would never state.

Bancroft invited Quist to have supper with him and Helen one evening and the two appeared to be putting themselves out to please, which as Quist told himself later, somewhat wryly, wasn't any effort on her part; all she had to do was be present and any healthy male would be pleased—providing said male didn't have other things on his mind. They'd tried to pump him regarding his progress in the Callister case, but Quist had nothing to offer.

The days dragged past, nor could Quist uncover anything new of importance, while he settled into a routine of sleeping and eating, and drinking at the Texas Bar, with impatient walks about town between times.

And then one morning, quite early, a westbound train brought the long-awaited reply from Jay Fletcher. Quist snatched it eagerly from the conductor's hand and with brief muttered thanks, hurried to the interior of the depot where he could read without interruption. Ripping open the envelope, he started eagerly to peruse the closely written report.

As his gaze flitted across the written lines dawning satisfaction appeared in his features. His topaz eyes glinted. Once his face clouded and he mentally excoriated himself. "Damn! I should have remembered where I heard that Jamison name. Something kept clicking in my mind all the while." By the time he'd finished reading and stuck the envelope in his pocket he was chuckling to himself, "I even hit the jackpot—got more than I'd hoped for."

He returned to the hotel and was the first guest at breakfast. That finished, he emerged to the street once more, and headed east along Main until he'd reached a store which bore a sign reading *John Daggert, Gunsmith*. Here, Quist opened the door and entered.

The shop wasn't large and gave the appearance of being cluttered. Various tools were scattered about a table. There was a can of oil, and one of grease. Another table held partially assembled firearms, bits of gun mechanisms and a few old weapons awaiting repair—or beyond repair. Gun barrels leaned against corners. Rifle and revolver butts were heaped in a box on the oil-stained floor. A glass case held new guns for sale; a second case was jammed with older weapons. At a bench, Daggert was engaged with a small file, working over a six-shooter ejector head, clamped in a small vise.

Daggert was an elderly man with stringy gray hair and a spare frame. His canvas apron was smeared with gun-grease and oil. There was a smudge of grease on one cheek as well. His gnarled fingers moved deftly with the file, which he put down when Quist entered. He beamed widely over rimless glasses which rested almost on the end of his nose. "Mr. Quist! I've been wondering if you'd drop in."

Quist stared at the man. "Say, I know you."

"Certain you do. I matched up a pair of forty-fours for you back in El Paso—pshaw! that's over nine years back. How you been?"

The two shook hands. "Missed you from the old place in El Paso," Quist said. "Somebody said you'd retired."

"Tried retirin'. Wore me out. Had to get back to work. I come here four years ago." They conversed a few minutes. Daggert asked if there was anything he could do for Quist.

"Maybe so," Quist replied. "You've probably heard what I'm doing here. All the rest of the town seems to know." He drew from his pocket the forty-four shell he'd found on the hotel gallery. "Now I'm not expecting the right answer to what I want to know, but there's just a chance that somebody has had a gun in here recently, which left that sort of firing-pin mark on it, and that you'd recognize it."

Daggert studied the shell, handed it back with a shake of the head. "That's like asking me to find a needle in a haystack." He smiled. "No, I can't re'lect anything of the kind. There's lots of forty-fours used hereabouts, both revolvers and rifles—"

"That's about what I expected," Quist nodded. The two conversed a few minutes longer and Quist was about ready to depart, when his eyes were caught by a rifle standing against Daggert's bench. "That," he observed admiringly, "is a handsome piece of workmanship. Forty-four?"

Daggert nodded and handed over the gun for Quist's inspection. "I'd be right proud to sell a gun like that, Mr. Quist. It's a real beautiful firearm, with that engraved barrel and the inlaid mother-of-pearl design in the butt. That butt's gen-u-wine rosewood. Silver mountings too. I ordered it special for Trenton, who owned the T-90 outfit, but he died real sudden—heart disease—before the gun arrived, so I got it on my hands. I figure to sell it to Everett Bancroft, over to the hotel, maybe."

"Bancroft figuring to buy it?"

"He was in here again last night lookin' at it. He's just like a kid lustin' after a red wagon, can't scarcely keep from runnin' in here to look at it, ever' so often. We been dickerin' quite a spell now. He wants to trade his present Winchester in on it, of course. That's all right, but I want twenty dollars to boot. Bancroft claims he can't afford it right now, and only offers ten. But I'll get him. At first he was only offering five and an old six-gun."

Quist looked thoughtful. "You know, Everett Bancroft has been right entertaining since I've been here. He and his sister, Helen, had me to supper a few nights ago. I'd like to do something for him." Quist placed a twenty-dollar gold-piece on the bench. "But I wouldn't want him to know I had anything to do with it. So there's the twenty you need to boot, and you can get another ten out of him, when you make the deal. Send him word you're ready to let him have the rifle."

Daggert eyed Quist narrowly. "You're on the trail of some-

174

thin', Mr. Quist. You don't need to shilly-shally with me. I know how to keep my mouth shut. All right, I'll send word to Bancroft, soon's you leave, to bring his Winchester and get his new gun."

Quist nodded. "When you get his old gun, slip in a cartridge and pull the trigger. Save the empty shell for me. I'll be around again, some time today. There'll be another gold-piece in it when you give me the shell."

Half an hour later, Quist dropped into the hotel bar, had a drink and left by way of the lobby. Helen Bancroft was behind the desk. "You acting as clerk today?" Quist asked.

"Temporarily, until Grimes can get dressed. Everett's gone to buy a new rifle. My grief! I've never seen a man so crazy about guns as Everett is. He was practically running when he left here."

Quist laughed. "Every man should have a hobby."

"That's no sign he should ride it to death." Helen sounded a bit snappish, and Quist departed after a few minutes' more talk.

He stood on the sidewalk a minute, staring east along Main Street, until he saw Everett Bancroft emerge from the gunsmith's shop, a new rifle cradled fondly in one arm. Quist left his position on the sidewalk and strolled over to the stagecoach stables. Alex was in her small office at one side. He talked a minute and ended up by asking to borrow her father's horse. Five minutes later he was in the saddle, guiding the big black animal across Main Street and into Mesquite. At the corral back of the hotel, he dismounted and tethered the horse beneath the roofed shelter. He took time enough to roll and smoke a cigarette, then sauntered casually down toward Daggert's gun shop. When he emerged a minute or so later he carried two empty shells in his pocket.

He started walking west again, speaking to one or two people who passed. He resisted the temptation to stop at the Texas Bar and pushed on until he'd reached his hotel again. He glanced into the lobby and saw Nelly Grimes behind the desk, looking very disgruntled.

Quist sauntered through the doorway, assumed a look of surprise. "What you doing now, Mr. Grimes, working the desk night and day both?"

Grimes looked his exasperation. "It begins to look like it, doesn't it? It just seems I hardly touch my head to my pillow, when Miss Helen has to wake me up. It's very upsetting."

"What happened to Bancroft? I thought he was day clerk."

"What do you suppose happened to him? A gun! He bought a new rifle and nothing would do but he must go out beyond the city limits and try it out. I tell you, Mr. Quist, I've just about reached the end of my rope. I've a good notion to resign."

"Not a bad idea maybe. Where's Miss Helen?"

"She's down to Perkins & Meek's General Store, making up the day's order. Nobody seems to care for my welfare. I haven't even had time to get a bite yet, and when I don't have my coffee almost the instant I'm out of bed, I'm ready to fly right off the handle. I just lose all sense of security." He paused and asked timidly, "Mr. Quist, will you be here for a few minutes? Well, then, would it be too much trouble to keep an eye on my desk while I slip into the kitchen and get a little snack to tide me over?"

"Go ahead, by all means. I doubt anyone will be coming in."

Grimes scurried from behind the desk and out through the dining room, at present empty. "This," Quist mused, "comes under the heading of being a dirty trick—but it's necessary." He drew from his pocket the small thirty-two revolver he had taken from Urban Jarrell and, reaching across the desk, drew out the hotel money drawer. Pushing back the top tray, he dropped the gun into the lower part, and reclosed the drawer.

When Grimes returned five minutes later, Quist was lounging against the desk and smoking a cigarette. He brushed aside

176

Grimes' thanks and asked, "Have you got two five-dollar bills for a ten, Mr. Grimes."

"I think so." Grimes pulled out his cash drawer, shoved back the coin tray at the top and reached beneath for the bills. Then he stopped abruptly, one hand frozen in mid-air. "Well, I never! If I don't give Everett a piece of my mind. It serves him right for accusing me. He probably had it himself all the time."

"What's up?"

"This—this gun." Grimes pointed one finger as though he were directing attention to a rattlesnake. "It was missing. I was accused of taking it. I wouldn't touch it. I don't like guns. They kill people—" He stopped suddenly.

Quist reached into the drawer and brought out the nickel-plated weapon. He examined it. One shell had been exploded. His face went suddenly grim. Grimes started to wilt beneath his steady gaze. Quist said, "The sheriff and his deputy were looking for a thirty-two. And with one shot exploded. This looks bad, Grimes. It was a thirty-two that was dug out of Miss Helen's door. Why did you want to shoot her? What has she got on you?"

Grimes' face was ashen. He clutched at the desk for support. "My—my gracious!" he half whispered. "Surely you don't think—"

"I guess you and I had best walk down to the sheriff's office," Quist said sternly.

"B-B-But, Mr. Quist, you're making a mistake—"

"Why did you want her out of the way—?" Grimes started a protest. Quist went on, his voice relentless, "This could mean a long term in prison, Grimes. The only way to save your skin is to talk, tell me what you know. First, it was just a matter of absconding. Now you've attempted murder—"

"Absconding?" Grimes sagged back against the cabinet of key slots, terror written plainly on his white face.

"Not going to try to deny it, are you, Grimes?" Quist laughed harshly. "I think you'd best come up to my room and we'll have a little talk. It's your only chance."

"Jus—just as you say, Mr. Quist."

Meekly, he followed Quist up the stairway.

XX

IT WAS the hottest part of the day. There weren't many people on the streets now. Men withdrew to the coolness of saloons; a few drowsed in the shadows between buildings or in chairs, tilted against walls. Horses at hitchracks stood slumped on three legs, heads down, tails switching reluctantly at droning flies. Resin bubbled from the plank sidewalks.

Everett Bancroft and Helen waited in the lobby of the hotel. Scarcely any breeze entered the half-open door. Bancroft was behind the desk, his new rifle standing in one corner. Helen spoke from an armchair against the wall, "I've racked my brains, but I can't see what Mr. Quist would have to say that's so important."

Bancroft shrugged. "Maybe he thinks he's discovered something that may alter the case one way or another." He smothered a yawn. "That damned Grimes! Where do you suppose he's gone? I could have gone out and shot a few more rounds."

The girl said, "Maybe you threatened him once too often. I've said time and again you've got to control your temper. I know Grimes better than you do. He has limits." She adjusted a bit of lace on one cuff, tucked in a few locks of stray blond hair.

"I know one thing," Bancroft said. "This vest—" referring to the fancy vest he wore—"is too hot. I'm going upstairs and take it off." He left the desk and mounted the flight of steps, Helen's questioning eyes following him until he'd disappeared. Within a few minutes he returned, wearing a dark coat over his white

178

shirt and black string tie. "That new repeater," he observed, "shoots like a charm. This morning I clipped the heads off three quail at fifty paces or thereabouts—"

The lobby door swung back. Alex Callister and Rod Larrabee entered. The two women eyed each other a moment and exchanged brief smiles. Rod said, "Greg said to meet him here. Isn't he—?"

Sheriff Kiernan came barging through the door, face running with perspiration. "All right, what's all this about? Where's Quist? He told me he'd be here and explain a few things. All poppycock, I reckon. The sooner that man leaves town the better for all of us. Miss Helen—" bowing and sweeping off his sombrero—"you look as sparkling as a spring day."

Helen smiled. "This heat seems to be dulling my sparkle."

"And you, Alex—" the sheriff mopped his face with a bandanna—"I've never seen you more titillatin'."

"Thank you, Jake. Have you any idea what Mr. Quist wants us—?"

"Mr. Quist will explain shortly," Quist stated, pushing through the doorway. He smiled genially. "Sorry to keep you waiting, but it was done purposely. I've a lot to say. I didn't want to be interrupted. With Miss Helen's permission we'll move back to the dining room. It's empty now and it's too early to prepare for the supper people. I've already investigated at the kitchen. The waitress has gone home and the cook is snoring as though he were already there."

"This sounds like a lot of nonsense, Quist," Kiernan boomed. "As sheriff of Pitahaya County, it's my duty to conduct any meeting to be held. Just give me your facts and I'll—"

"I'll give you the facts, Sheriff," Quist interposed coldly. "Just keep your lip buttoned and listen."

Kiernan commenced an indignant sputtering, but Helen placed one hand on his arm. "Let's do as Mr. Quist suggests, Jake, and get this business settled as soon as possible."

They filed into the deserted dining room and headed toward the far corner of the outer wall. Light came through windows at the rear of the building. Cloths and accessories had been removed from the wooden tables. Chairs were pulled out and turned around. Finally they were seated, Quist situated where he could face the others. Alex took a chair behind a table in the extreme corner, with Larrabee and Jake Kiernan on each side of her. Immediately next to the sheriff sat Helen Bancroft—Kiernan had maneuvered it that way—and to Helen's left, chair facing Quist, was Everett Bancroft. Quist rolled and lighted a cigarette while Kiernan fumed.

Quist began, "I believe you're all aware that I stated a double murder had taken place the night Callister and his wife died. I'm now ready to offer proof of my statement. It's taken time to dig up the facts I wanted, but I've had help from other operatives of the T.N. & A.S., whose word is to be relied on. They're very thorough and their investigation has touched at points in Missouri, Louisiana and Utah, as well as one or two other places—"

"For cripes' sake, Quist," Kiernan growled, "get on with it. I'm a busy man. I can't waste time listenin' to you spiel about your blasted railroad—"

Helen interrupted, "Take it easy, Jake. We owe it to Mr. Quist to at least listen courteously."

"Helen's right, Jake," Bancroft put in.

Quist thanked them and resumed, "Suppose I start by mentioning an outfit known as Texas Jack's Wild West Show and Exhibition. Sort of a circus, I suppose, copied after Bill Cody's show, that traveled around the country, featuring sharpshooters, bronc riders, Indians—that sort of thing. It's out of business now, I understand. You've all heard of it. I feel sure a couple of you have been present at performances. One of the stars of the show was a man named Ed Jamison—incidentally on my stage ride here I overheard a drummer mention him, so he's not been forgotten. The drummer claimed he was the best shot he'd ever

180

seen. Broke glass balls with a forty-four instead of using a shotgun, like a lot of sharpshooters. Did other fancy shooting too, I've learned since. Dead-eye Ed, he was billed as—something like that. The Nonpareil. Two performances daily—" Quist laughed softly. "I could even show you one of the old advertising dodgers. It made me real enthusiastic, and I wished I knew something about guns—"

"All right, Mr. Quist," Everett Bancroft said quietly, concern showing in his face, "you don't have to prolong it."

"The name Jamison mean something to you?" Quist asked.

The man known as Bancroft nodded. "I'm Ed Jamison," he confessed. He added wryly, "A man takes a new name, tries to make a fresh start in life and then something interrupts, and—but now I'm interrupting. I'll admit freely I'm not Helen's brother so—"

"Look here, Bancroft—Jamison—whatever your name is," the sheriff bellowed, "if you're wanted by the law—"

"I'm not," Bancroft-Jamison said curtly. "Let Mr. Quist continue, please."

From the others there'd been no word. Alex and Rod were curiously eyeing the man. Helen Bancroft sat, eyes down, as though sensing what was coming. Quist said, "Thanks, Jamison. You've saved time by not making foolish denials." He went on, "Another star of the Texas Jack show was billed as Helene, the Blond Centauress. She was also a crack shot, breaking glass balls, shooting the necks from bottles, knocking the spots from playing cards. Some of it she did from a running horse, too. I assure you, she was good. And beautiful the advertising said. I'll agree with the advertising."

Helen Bancroft forced a wan smile. "So long as Ed has confessed, I suppose I may as well admit to being the Helene you mention."

"My thanks to you, Miss Helen." Quist bowed.

"I'll be damned!" Kiernan blurted, staring at Helen Bancroft.

"It was only natural, I suppose," Quist continued, "that a romance take place between the Nonpareil and the Blond Centauress—until Ed Jamison met another woman who had joined the show as a sort of wardrobe mistress. She too had charms. And it was she Ed Jamison married. I'm told he was deeply in love. And insanely jealous. During a jealous fit of rage, he killed another man—"

"And I'd do it again," Bancroft-Jamison said doggedly. "He wouldn't leave her alone. Quist, I'll save more time. Right, I killed Carter Morse—that was his name—and went to the penitentiary for it. I served my sentence and was released."

"True," Quist nodded. "Jamison, I think you owe it to yourself also to state that Carter Morse pulled his gun first. Where's your wife now, Jamison?"

"She—she died some time back." The man swallowed hard. He didn't look at Quist for a moment.

"You spoke truth that time too," Quist said softly.

Helen broke in, "Is all this necessary, Mr. Quist? Ed thought a lot of his wife, and to rake up old memories—"

Jamison interrupted, "That's neither here nor there. What I want to know is who killed Anne, if she didn't commit suicide?"

"Getting impatient, Jamison?" Quist asked. "I realize this is a strain, but it's ridiculous for you to ask who killed Anne. *You* did, of course."

XXI

THERE WAS a sudden pregnant silence. Jamison's jaw dropped. He could only stare at Quist, unable for the moment to speak. The words came with an effort when he finally said, "Up to a certain point, Mr. Quist, you've been right, but now your investigations have led you astray—"

182

"I don't believe so," Quist snapped. "Sheriff, you'd best take his gun."

Kiernan stared open-mouthed at both men. "I think you're crazy, Quist. You and your detectin'—"

"Get his gun!" Quist snapped.

Kiernan jumped and started to stumble from his chair. Jamison rose from his seat, opened his coat and held it back. "I'm not armed. My cartridge belt and six-shooter are up in my room—"

"You see, Quist?" the sheriff growled. He resumed his seat.

"That was a mistake," Quist said flatly.

Helen said impatiently, "You've accused Ed, Mr. Quist, of killing Anne, so I suppose he killed Vance Callister too."

"Now you know better than that, Miss Helen," Quist said reprovingly. "You see I've had an opportunity to talk with Nelly Grimes. I've put two and two together."

"This gets crazier all the time," Jamison protested. "I don't know what Grimes has told you, but he's already sworn at the inquest that Helen and I were both at the hotel that evening. If you know where Grimes is—he's disappeared temporarily—"

"I know where he is."

Jamison had remained on his feet, a few paces from Quist. "Well, get him here then."

Quist shook his head. "Nelly Grimes lives in deadly fear of you, Jamison. He knows too much about you, and he saw what happened to Randall—"

"You're blaming me for Dodge Randall's death?" Jamison's jaw dropped, his eyes bulged.

Quist said, "I'd expect acting from a former showman, of course, but I'm not going to swallow it, Jamison."

"Keep still, Ed, let's hear this story to the end. I've got to get through here," Helen said, "and give orders to the cook. Go on, Mr. Quist, only hurry please."

Quist nodded. "We'll go back to the time when Jamison was jailed for that killing of Carter Morse. All three of you left the

Texas Jack show, Jamison to enter the Utah pen. One other left with you, a very friendly little man who had a deep attraction for the blond Helene. You were short of money but this little man had no compunctions about taking the show's money. He'd served as ticket seller and cashier with the show. Oh, yes, his name was Grimes, and there's still an absconding charge over his head when the authorities can locate him. I'm surprised he never took an alias."

Quist paused to roll and light a cigarette, while the others waited, tense. "Helene went to Baton Rouge where she got into what she called the hotel business. Quite a place you had, Miss Helen, a little gambling and a few other things we'll not mention. Anyway, the police closed you up, and you came here. Grimes came later and you gave him a job as night clerk. Jamison's wife went to St. Louis where she gave it out she was a governess in a girls' school. Actually, she was in charge of the linen and similar matters. As a former wardrobe mistress she probably was capable enough on the job. But she insisted on coming out here, Miss Helen, when she heard you had another hotel. Maybe the fact that you thought you were about to marry the wealthy Vance Callister urged her to such a move—"

Helen looked at him, tight-lipped. "Once more you're right," she conceded bitterly. "Anne has always wanted anything I wanted, and she's generally managed to get it too, worse luck. To be frank, Mr. Quist, there wasn't too much love lost between Anne and myself. But you've still failed to prove murder charges."

"I'll get to it. You wanted to marry Callister for his money, so as not to lose your hotel. You weren't doing as well as you expected. Meanwhile, Anne managed to work herself into Callister's graces when she turned him against you. So you worked it out between you. Ed Jamison was in prison. You thought he'd be there a long time. Let Anne marry Callister and then slowly poison him with arsenic. Then you'd divide the money. Right?"

184

"I know nothing of Anne's actions," Helen stated doggedly. "Maybe you're right. She was a little double-crosser."

Larrabee broke in, "You sure of all this, Greg?"

"I'm sure, Rod. So there's the setup. Jamison is in prison, cellmate to Dodge Randall. Randall is due to get out. Jamison tells him to go to Arcanum City and Helen will give him any money he needs, if he's up against it. Then, not too long after, Jamison is paroled, on condition he get a job in Salt Lake City. He writes Helen and Anne to that effect. They write and tell him to stay there and explain that Anne is going to marry Callister and all the rest of it. I've said that Jamison was insanely jealous. When he heard the plans he wrote a wild letter stating he'd kill Anne if she went through a marriage ceremony with Callister—"

"That's a lot of nonsense," Jamison snapped angrily. "I'm not going to stand here and listen—"

"You'll stay!" Quist rasped. "Rod, if he makes a move toward that door, stop him!" Jamison sank, glowering, back in his chair.

Quist went on, "And it's not nonsense, Jamison. Grimes saw the letter, once, when Helen wasn't in her room. I tricked Grimes into telling me a lot of things, but he was glad to ease his conscience. Absconding with money is one thing; murder quite another. I had a horse ready, back of the hotel, and I sent Grimes out to the Box-VC, to stay until he's needed to testify. So you can't gun him out of existence—"

Jamison forced a smile that was half snarl. "You're just crazy!"

Quist ignored the remark. "So Anne went ahead and married Callister despite Jamison's threats. As soon as he heard it, Jamison came here, after breaking parole, and posed as Helen's brother. He still threatened to kill Anne. Helen tried to pacify him, but suddenly that night she noticed he'd left the hotel. That brought things to a head. Helen was thinking of Callister's and Anne's wills. If Anne died first, the money would never get into Helen's hands. Right, Helen?"

"You've certainly got a fertile imagination, Mr. Quist," Helen said coolly.

"Backed up by facts, Miss Helen. With Jamison's horse missing from the shelter back of the hotel, you guessed immediately where he'd gone. But Alex Callister's pony stood there. You couldn't afford to waste time. Grimes could take care of hotel affairs in your absence—which same might not even be noticed. And he could swear an alibi for you later—you and Jamison. So you mounted Alex's horse, just as you were, and highlined it after Jamison. Probably cut across country without following the trail to the Box-VC. A horse can travel through country that would stop a wagon, too, so there'd be little chance of meeting anyone."

"Rave on, Mr. Quist," the woman said carelessly. "It's a very interesting deduction, but you can't prove a thing."

Quist said, "I'm not through with the story yet, Miss Helen. I figure you arrived at the Box-VC just as Jamison pulled trigger, from his position near that cottonwood to the north of the house, and sent his shot through the window of the Callister bedroom. Maybe they had just started to undress for bed. Jamison, it requires damn' good shooting to judge a target through a pane of glass—shooting worthy of a top marksman. But you did it. Next, you shot Callister—"

"That's a lie!" Jamison blurted excitedly. "It was Helen killed Callister. She jerked the rifle from my hand the instant I'd ejected my shell. I saw Anne stagger back and Callister jumped for the window like he was going to draw the shade when Helen—" He halted suddenly, sick confusion spreading across his features. Helen shot him a look of mingled consternation and reproach.

Quist smiled thinly. "Sucker," he said quietly. "Grimes had suspected that from things you and Helen dropped, but now I have it from your own lips." He faced the others. "So there's the situation. Jamison killed Anne. Helen killed Callister. Helen's a smart woman. She had sense enough to think fast, in a try for the money she hopes to inherit. She just grabbed the rifle from

Jamison, fired, ejected the shell in case another shot was necessary—"

"That's not true," Helen protested. "I know things look bad—"

Quist cut in. "Very bad. There's still sign to be seen in the vicinity of that cottonwood. Prints of a man and woman, horses. Iverson happens to be right friendly with those Mexicans west of town. One of them told the Doc he saw Helen riding furiously into town that night, coming in by way of Mesquite Street. But she didn't ride all the way to the hotel but dismounted a block away and let the horse run free. Kiernan picked it up later. Then she re-entered the hotel by the kitchen. For all anyone knew, she'd been in her room until she reappeared. But before leaving the Box-VC she'd given Jamison instructions, to arrange things to look as if Anne had killed Callister and then shot herself. So the bedroom light was blown out and the bodies carried to the main room. Callister's six-shooter was placed in Anne's hand."

"Why—" Alex frowned—"weren't they left in the bedroom?"

"There was a broken pane of glass there, and it might have set a *smart* sheriff thinking the shots had come from outside." Quist darted a look at Kiernan's red face. "So the whole pane was pushed from the sash, to make it less noticeable from the outside, and the shade drawn and tacked down on the inside. It isn't likely that the sheriff more than glanced into the bedroom, anyway—if that. Rugs were thrown over the bloodstained carpet. I had the broken pieces of glass in my room, but someone lifted 'em. However, Nelly Grimes got them for me from Miss Helen's room."

Helen remained silent, head down, but Quist sensed she wasn't through yet. She'd think of something. Smart woman, Helen. Too smart.

Quist continued. "The Callister gun had to be placed in Anne's dead hand. But, also, two empty shells had to be placed in its cylinder to account for the two shots presumably fired from it. It was a forty-four caliber, as was Jamison's rifle. The guns are made to take the same cartridges. So the shells ejected from the rifle were substituted for two loads in Callister's six-shooter. Likely it didn't take long for Jamison to exchange the two exploded ejects—"

"Look here, Greg," Rod interposed, "why didn't Jamison just fire two shots from Callister's six-shooter?"

"They'd fired two shots. More might have been risky. Jamison had to have time to arrange things. For all he knew, Box-VC riders might be nearing the ranch. Actually, Stovepipe was on the road. Maybe Jamison heard him. You can hear a team and wagon a long way on a still night—especially if it has squeaky wheels. We know Jamison was hurried, because he was still hidden in the house when Stovepipe found the bodies. Stovepipe gave it small thought at the time, but now he's sure he heard a noise like a boot scraping, or some such careless move. After Stovepipe lit out for town again, Jamison completed tacking the shade in place. Eventually he left and reappeared at the hotel, making fast time across country and not following the road. When Kiernan and Iverson arrived, the scene was all set to look like murder and suicide. It's only natural to figure the suicide is last to die. Helen and Jamison figured the money was practically in their hands, with Helen heiring Anne's estate."

"You'll have a tough time proving this," Jamison grated. "If I said anything that implicated Helen you misunderstood. We'll hire good lawyers—another thing, who's going to believe Grimes' testimony? He's a thief, wanted by the law right now—"

"Chop it," Quist snapped. "So that's how things stood when Doc Iverson upset things by stating that Anne had died first. So, Grimes told me, Jamison and Helen were right perturbed. Drastic action was needed. I believe, Jamison, it was you who fired that forty-four slug at Iverson, to close his mouth, but I haven't felt it necessary to prove it. Next, Jamison got Randall to go to Black Ore Springs and hire three thugs to make a roadblock and waylay the stage and then kidnap Alex Callister. I hate to think what further was planned. I happened to take the stage that morning. The attempt failed. The three thugs—Biggs, Arden and Yoakum—have confessed and implicated Randall. So you see—"

"I'm not accountable for Randall's actions," Jamison said.

"T'hell you aren't," Quist snapped. "Anyway, when I arrived here, I examined the exploded shells in Callister's six-shooter. I realized then something funny was going on. The firing-pin indentations in two of them were vastly different than the mark of the empty shell on which the hammer rested, so I figured those two had come from a different gun, and had been inserted in the cylinder for a purpose. I stuck one fingertip in the end of the gun-barrel. It came out oily. The gun hadn't been fired since its last cleaning. Later I examined the rooms at the ranch house and pieced together a story there. It was then I announced that instead of Anne killing Callister, double murder had been done that night."

Quist dropped his cigarette, put his toe on it. "Some time back when it was nosed around town I might come here, Jamison wrote me, asking me to come and conduct an investigation here. Intended for a shrewd move, I suppose. If I discovered anything pointing to Jamison, I might disregard it. Who'd dream of a murderer asking for his own investigation. But that move failed. Extreme measures were necessary. A shot was fired into Helen's door. That was something that might be called an accident, but Grimes fell under suspicion because he had a thirty-two gun in his cash drawer. Jamison began threatening him, thinking Grimes was about to go over to Alex's side. Jamison and Helen became nervous. Randall was ordered to hire somebody to put me out of the way. Hunk Worden tried and failed. Then I went after Randall, intending only to wound him and then persuade him to tell what he knew. But Jamison ended Randall's life with a forty-four slug, to keep his mouth shut."

"By God, you can't prove I did it!" Jamison sounded outraged.

189

An icy smile touched Quist's lips, but there was nothing of humor in his topaz eyes. "It's already proved, Jamison. When you traded in for your new rifle, I got an exploded shell from the old Winchester, through John Daggert. The firing-pin mark on the shell is identical with a shell I found on the upper gallery the night Randall was shot to death. You had merely stepped out on the gallery from your room, fired once and hastened back. And those two shells exactly match the two suspected shells in Vance Callister's six-shooter. So I guess you and Helen are pretty well tied up."

Helen forced a short, harsh laugh. "Not a bad story, Mr. Quist —though I'm not admitting I'm guilty. Nor Ed either. Money will provide good lawyers for our defense. And I still have a good chance of heiring what Callister willed to his wife, Anne, unless it can be proved that Anne died first—"

Quist shook his head, a certain pity in his eyes for the woman. "Don't try to pull the wool over my eyes with that one, Helen. It won't go down. In the first place, Anne wasn't Callister's legal wife. She was still married to Ed Jamison. In the second place, any reputable doctor who listens to Doc Iverson will know that Anne died first, and will confirm Iverson's conclusions."

Alex and Rod looked their amazement. Kiernan sat dumb, jaw hanging, looking from Helen to Jamison and back to Helen again, unable to find words.

Jamison's eyes were downcast, he shifted uneasily in his chair and stuck one hand in his pocket.

Helen started to speak, then stopped. Disappointment, fear, frustration, were written plainly in her dark eyes. She lifted one protesting hand as though to ward off further accusations. "I— I feel faint," she gasped, and sagged against Jake Kiernan.

Kiernan lifted his left arm and put it around her shoulders.

Quist said sharply, "Watch it, Kiernan!"

But Helen's right hand had already swept across the sheriff's knees, reaching to the six-shooter in his holster, jerking it out. Wrenching away, she tossed it on the table near Jamison.

"Grab it, Ed!" she cried. "We can still fight our way out. There're horses in the shelter back—"

Kiernan, grunting in surprise, swore, lurched toward Helen to retrieve his gun and knocked her in front of Jamison who was just pulling trigger on the revolver he carried in his right coat pocket. Smoke and flame erupted through the cloth, ripping into Helen's body, as Jamison sought to reach the sheriff's gun.

Quist was already on his feet, moving swiftly to one side, left hand jerking back the lapel of his coat while his right flashed to the underarm Colt in its holster. A breeze from Jamison's second shot fanned Quist's cheek, even as his own gun was jumping in his hand—once, twice, three times.

Quist's leaden slugs slammed Jamison back against the table. He huddled there a moment, a gun in each hand, fighting to bring them to bear on Quist. Quist fired a fourth time.

Quite suddenly, Jamison pitched forward on his face, as a weapon dropped from each hand to clatter on the board floor.

Powdersmoke swirled through the room, stinging eyes and throat and nostrils. Dust was still sifting down from the rafters overhead, shaken by the detonation of the heavy weapons.

Quist was already plugging out empty shells and shoving fresh loads in his cylinder. His voice sounded unusually loud in the sudden silence after the thundering of the guns. "Rod, get Alex out of here. There'll be people clamoring around in a minute. Take care of it. Kiernan and I will handle things here."

Larrabee hurried Alex from the room. Already excited voices were heard in the lobby and on the street. Quist turned back and glanced at the two bodies sprawled on the floor. Kiernan was just retrieving his six-shooter from a point just beyond Jamison's outstretched fingers. Thin smoke rose from the smoldering spot in Jamison's pocket.

"He—he had a gun—in his pocket," the sheriff blurted dumbly. "Miss Helen got in front of him just as he fired—"

"I knew it," Quist said irritably. "I saw the weighty bulge in his coat pocket when he threw it back to show you he wasn't wearing a ca'tridge belt and gun. But he convinced you. I said at the time it was a mistake, but you didn't catch on—"

He broke off and stooped near Helen's body. After a minute he moved away, muttering something to do with being glad the bullet hadn't hit her face. He crouched near Jamison's side, examining swiftly the destruction wrought by his underarm forty-four. Kiernan said, "Should I tell Rod to go for the doctor?"

Quist shook his head. "Nothing here that a doctor could cure."

"Finished—both of 'em?"

"Finished complete."

"You're pretty fast, Mr. Quist, getting that gun out—"

Quist snapped savagely, "In your eyes that makes me something special, I suppose. Damn and blast killing and the people who make it possible!"

The sheriff stared at him open-mouthed. He didn't say anything. Quist scowled down toward the floor a moment, then asked, "You can handle things here, can't you?"

"Yeah, sure. Where you going?"

"I've got to get down to the depot and wire my boss that I've just sewed up another bloodstained right-of-way for the company." He started toward the door.

Kiernan said awkwardly, "I reckon I owe you an apology, Mr. Quist."

Quist growled, "Forget it, Jake. We all make mistakes. Hell's bells on a tomcat! I was even suspicioning you for a spell."

"Me! Of murder?" Kiernan looked dumbfounded, his jaw dropped, his eyes bugged out. "Now why in Gawd's name should you have ever suspicioned *me*—Sheriff of Pitahaya County?"

"I'm beginning to wonder myself," Quist said wearily, "after seeing you in action."